THIS IS
Our LOVE

THIS IS
Our LOVE

With Contributions from 16 Recording Artists

ENGAGING THE NEEDS OF OUR WORLD THROUGH WORSHIP

To download chord sheets for these songs visit www.jodycross.com
or for more information on this project visit www.churches.worldvision.ca/thisisourlove

© 2012 by World Vision Canada

Published by **World Vision Canada, Church Engagement Division**
1 World Drive, Mississauga, ON L5T 2Y4

In partnership with **Crossroads Christian Communications**
1295 North Service Rd., Burlington, ON

Contents

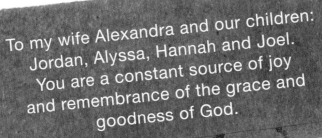

To my wife Alexandra and our children:
Jordan, Alyssa, Hannah and Joel.
You are a constant source of joy
and remembrance of the grace and
goodness of God.

Acknowledgements

Having, by the grace and mercy of God, been in Christian ministry for nearly 25 years, I am grateful to have learned much from many people: pastors, mentors, speakers, worship leaders, teachers, family and friends. All of these have been used of God and His Spirit to shape my thinking and my passions. I am committed to being a lifelong learner, and in the past few years I have been compelled to pass on what the Lord has been teaching me.

God's surprises come when we least expect them. Through a developing relationship with World Vision Canada, I had a series of conversations with their National Church Ambassador, Don Moore, about what could be done to encourage believers and local churches to grow in their love for God and their love for those in need. Don presented me with the idea of using music and worship to stir believers. Don's vision, energy, and enthusiasm for this concept was infectious, and as we continued to dialogue and dream, the project grew in its scope. Don watched for signs of God's hand leading and blessing us and confidently moved forward with the process, one step at a time. He believed that I was someone who could lead this project and I am grateful for his support and confidence in me.

World Vision Canada approached Crossroads Christian Communications as a project partner and they both have been enthusiastically behind the idea of providing believers with something that would both encourage and challenge Christ followers to live their worship with a heart of mercy and justice. I have been blessed to partner with both World Vision Canada and Crossroads on the *This Is Our Love* project. Before you is an end result that began with many conversations about how to use a breadth of music, testimony and God's Word to create a devotional resource that will, we hope, inform, inspire, and move people to action. The World Vision Canada team, Project Director Don Moore and Project Manager Ron Weber have provided immense help and support in bringing the project from concept to reality. The Crossroads team, Gary Gerrard, Bruce Stacey and George McEachern added valuable insights and much energy for this project. I am grateful for each of these leaders and the organizations they serve. Thank you to Ellen Graf-Martin, Erika Bartos and the team at Graf-Martin Communications. You have captured the heartbeat of this project and translated it beautifully into image and design. Thank you as well to Rose Collins, copy editor, for taking these words and sentences and making them flow as they should.

We tapped into the heart springs of many singers / songwriters across Canada. Thank you to each artist who wrestled with the issue of worship and justice and took the time to flesh it out in song and in their lives. I am grateful to all those who submitted songs in the initial phase of selecting songs. I am grateful to the panel of selection judges from across the country who took the time to carefully consider each song and select the ones they felt best met the project criteria. Thank you to the 15 artists, bands and management whose songs were selected for the project. Thank you for your excellence in ministry and artistry and for partnering with World Vision and Crossroads. You have caught our vision for what this resource could become and you have shared your heart in your songs.

Thank you to Travis Doucette and Drew Brown for their musical contributions to the song "This is Our Love." Who knew what would become of this song and where it would go! Thank you to the Evans for your hospitality in allowing us a creative space to write that day. Thank you to Drew Brown for his musical shaping of the song and for lending his voice.

Andrew Horrocks, of AME Studios in Kitchener, recorded and produced the song, "This is Our Love" and mastered the entire CD project. Thank you Andrew for embracing the vision and bringing it to life with your expertise and creative abilities.

Through the process of creating this project, I have been nurtured in the Word of God by Pastor Paul Carter and the ministry of First Baptist Church in Orillia, Ontario. You have caught the vision of ministering to the least and caring for the lost, and have inspired me to press deeper in my own life and ministry to do the same. Thank you to all of you who I am privileged to serve with in ministry at First Baptist. You have stood with me in ministry both inside and outside the walls of our fellowship.

To our children, Jordan, Alyssa, Hannah and Joel: as you grow, may you find in God's infinite grace and salvation the reason to pour out your life and love for others' good and His glory. I am so blessed in having a very special life partner and confidante: my wife Alexandra. Alex, you have consistently cheered me on in this process, believing in me and in the project as I followed God and His creative call. I see such mercy and selflessness displayed in your life and I cherish the gift you have.

Finally, all praise and thanks to our Lord Jesus Christ who has drawn me to Himself and poured out His gifts of undeserved goodness and mercy. In my pursuit of You, Lord, and by Your work in me, may Your heart beat inside mine and move me to love and live as You did.

Jody Cross

Foreword

Canada has been blessed with a wealth of gifted musicians who are passionate about Christ and about creating music that challenges and encourages the Church in its mission. This unique devotional book and CD compilation was born from the intuition that there was a common strain emerging from the music of Canadian contemporary worship artists and musicians – that of compassion for the impoverished and justice for the marginalized.

This is why World Vision Canada and Crossroads Christian Communications were excited to partner together in producing *This is Our Love* under the leadership of Dr. Jody Cross. Those of us involved in this project are committed to meeting the physical and spiritual needs of those around us, both locally and globally.

Confident that God is, in fact, using those He has gifted with music and art to give voice to His heart of passion for "the least of these," we purposed to help amplify this voice. We've collected 16 of the most highly valued Canadian worship songs that focus on compassion for the poor and marginalized. Based on the music and lyrics of these songs, Dr. Cross has crafted devotional writings that will connect with individuals and groups alike, sparking in us greater acts of love for His Kingdom's sake.

We want to thank the 60 artists who submitted over 90 songs for consideration on this project, and the nation-wide selection committee of worship and ministry leaders (listed in the appendix) who helped narrow the 33 finalists down to these top 16 songs. It was certainly a challenge to choose from the wealth of contributions. We fully believe that the songs chosen are a compelling and truthful representation of what God is asking of His Church, and we're very thankful to have the opportunity of presenting them to you.

Our hope is that many Canadian churches will embrace and incorporate these songs into their worship repertoire as a reminder of our mission. But more than that, as this CD and devotional guide make very clear, our greatest hope is that our worship will inspire each of us to courageously step into partnering with Christ in active lives of selfless love, so that His Kingdom will continue to be built on earth as it is in heaven.

Don Moore
NATIONAL CHURCH AMBASSADOR

World Vision Canada

Bruce Stacey
CHIEF CONTENT OFFICER

Crossroads Christian
Communications, Inc.

Introduction

The News of the Gospel

Bad news: once all of us were enemies of God, dead in our sin, and without hope. **Good news:** God in His rich mercy saw our condition, heard our cry and sent His Son to redeem us. **Best news:** by grace through faith we are made alive in Christ and given new hope and eternal life. **Today's news:** people everywhere are waiting to find hope that is in Jesus Christ and we are the messengers.

Do you remember those first days of "new hope" in your life when you came to faith in Jesus? The unbelievable joy? Those first experiences of worship? The complete shift in perspective that your new life was now all about loving and serving Him?

There really are no words to describe what it's like to begin to taste and see the depths of the goodness, love, and grace of God. For me that happened on a warm August evening over thirty years ago. I'm sure you can also remember the growing urgency you felt, in those early days, to then turn and give back out of the overflow of God's love for you.

Out of this love we are called and compelled to respond to Him, in love and in worship. We all know worship is more than a music thing and more than a Sunday morning event. **Worship is a lifestyle involving all we are and all we do, all the time.** A life of worship seeks to bring glory to God in everything we do *(1 Corinthians 10:31)*. Worship is about what happens behind closed doors with us and God, what happens in the context of the gathered community of faith in corporate worship, and what happens "out there," in the real world. **What does it mean to live out a life of worship beyond the walls of our sanctuaries?** There are so many who have not yet encountered Christ's love. At home and around the world there are so many that live in the grips of poverty. The Word and Spirit of God convict us that there is much more to worship than just "What can I get out of it?" This gift we've been given is meant to be shared.

> This gift we've been given is meant to be shared.

Freely Received

We live in a time and place of unprecedented abundance. We know firsthand the blessings of material provision, and, most importantly, we have experienced the spiritual blessings of being in a saving relationship with Jesus Christ. How easy it is to forget the immeasurable mercy we have received. Living in "the Christian cocoon" we become forgetful of our broken life, and the magnificence of the grace of Christ that rescued us.

We are reminded of the words of Jesus in *Matthew 10:8, "Freely you have received, freely give."* We really like the first part of this verse, that nice phrase about receiving freely. But that second part, the "give" part is quite foreign, actually, to our deeply engrained ways of thinking and living. As consumeristic North Americans we are, tragically, very skilled at wanting and getting, but not so good at giving. We love to swim in a sea of blessing, and yet can't see that we are drowning in the waters of selfishness. We hear the Holy Spirit call us out of our bondage to self and "stuff:" "You have freely received, now freely give." God is stirring up His Church to be givers of all the goodness He has poured out. God's people are to be conduits of blessing, not reservoirs of it.

Freely Give

A journey is before us. It's a journey into unfamiliar territory, a journey to make our worship more authentic as we live out His love. It's a journey back to where we once were. It's a journey to "out there" to the sick, the widow, the broken, the poor, the needy, the lost, the fatherless, the least and the last.

The disciples were presented with an overwhelming task when Jesus called them to feed the hungry multitudes on the hillside. The disciples had very little food or money, but Jesus commanded them to give

> God's people are to be conduits of blessing, not reservoirs of it.

the masses something to eat *(John 6:37)*. Now, as in that moment, the task seems impossible. And just like in that moment, Jesus places the responsibility back on our shoulders. We look at the great need, we look at the complexity of the problem, and then we look at what we have, and, like Andrew, we feel that the need is so great but we have very little. Jesus always takes what we have and, when it is surrendered to His purposes, it is always enough to meet the need. He is always enough for us, for our task, and for those who desperately need Him.

Starting Out

Maybe you are like me, convicted, compelled, but fearful and unsure how to begin this going and giving, this doing justice and loving kindness.

What do we do? Where do we start? We ask our Heavenly Father to help us. We seek to be transformed by Him, and we call upon the Spirit of God to empower our witness and work in His world.

This is our love, to obey His commands. This is our love, to be filled with His love and take it beyond our own experience and enjoyment. This is our love, to take our worship outside the safe haven of our sanctuaries. His love at work in and through us is our journey. This project has been created with the hope that you will be encouraged to passionately and obediently live out the Great Commandments of loving God with all you are and loving your neighbour as yourself.

Are you ready to get started? Before you is a collection of songs by artists who have been compelled to respond to God's call of being worshipers who seek to do justice and love mercy. These 16 songs cover a variety of experiences and expressions. Accompanying each song is a chapter devoted to telling the story behind the songs, from the perspective of the artists. Each chapter contains firsthand accounts of the heart behind the song and the biblical perspective that undergirds the message. At the conclusion of each chapter is an offered prayer meant to aid you in expressing your heart to God. The discussion questions are meant to help you or your small group talk through the issues raised by the song and chapter. Finally, next steps are suggested to help you begin to walk out love and mercy in obedience to God's Word.

As you embark on this journey of discovering the heart of God for the broken, it is my prayer that the Spirit of God will transform your heart and challenge you to take ever greater steps of obedience in living out His mercy.

Jody Cross

To download chord sheets for these songs visit www.jodycross.com

This is Our Love

For the world You loved, for the world You came
For the world You gave Your life away
For the least of these
For the lost in need
For the last You gave Your life away

This is our song of love
This is our offering
We give our lives away

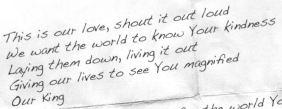

This is our love, shout it out loud
We want the world to know Your kindness
Laying them down, living it out
Giving our lives to see You magnified
Our King

For the world You loved, for the world You came
For the world You gave Your life away
For the least of these
For the lost in need
For the last You gave Your life away

This is our song of love,
To broken hearts we sing
We give our lives away

God of justice and mercy, let Your kingdom come
God of justice and mercy, let Your will be done

Jody Cross, Travis Doucette and Drew Brown

This is Our Love

By this we know love, that he laid down his life for us, and we ought to lay down our lives for the brothers. – 1 John 3:16

A Blank Cheque

One of the Bible's most well known verses of Scripture concerning worship can be found in *Romans 12:1*. The Apostle Paul commands us to present our bodies as a living sacrifice, holy and acceptable to God, which is our spiritual worship. **Worship is a response of remembrance that is fully conscious of the mercies of God.** In other words, because of all Jesus has done in our redemption; because we are justified by faith and saved by grace, we are to worship God by laying down our lives. Like Isaac on the altar, like Jesus on the cross, a life of worship is a life laid down, for the purposes and glory of God.

As a young pastor, I was mentored by a senior leader who exhorted me to completely surrender my life to the purposes of God. The analogy he used was that of a blank cheque. He challenged me to sign the cheque, address it to the Lord and leave the amount blank. God would direct me, he said, and do with my life what He intended. In the past 30 years of walking with the Lord, I have been so grateful for His grace that has faithfully led and kept me through all the assignments I've been given.

Compelled by God's World

Part of my journey as a pastor, worship leader and artist has been to write songs, specifically congregational worship songs. I have found that songs arrive in different ways. A verse of Scripture might jump off the page at me or a pregnant phrase in a sermon might grab me and compel me to write. The song "This is Our Love" came out of my time reflecting on a yearly theme selected by the local church where I was serving. The theme was, "Laying it Down, Living it Out." The companion verse was *1 John 3:16: "By this we know love, that he laid down his life for us, and we ought to lay down our lives for the brothers."*

I was compelled by this phrase, rich with biblical imagery, clearly speaking to what it means to be a worshiper of God. I was compelled to be that kind of Christ-follower, to lay my life down on His altar as a loving sacrifice. My hope was that our congregation might have one voice as we sought to be God's people in laying down our lives for each other, the least and the lost.

Songs often begin in moments of inspiration but are finished with hours of perspiration. I had the inspiration from the verse and then needed to do the hard work of actually crafting the song. I prayed that I might receive from the Lord what He had for me. Songwriters are stewards, receiving the trust from God and using the gift of anointed song for His glory, to teach, encourage and mobilize the Church.

As "This is Our Love" was written, I reflected on why Jesus came and whom He came for. The why: because of His obedience to God the Father. And for whom? **As He walked the dusty roads of Palestine, Jesus dem-**

onstrated over and over that He was there for the lost and broken. He touched the untouchable, healed the hopeless, and called the rejected. Jesus' love was a love in action. He lived love, spoke it, and ultimately gave up His life because of it.

But when the kindness and love of God our Savior appeared, he saved us, not because of righteous things we had done, but because of his mercy.

Titus 3:4-5a

We know love because it is written across the pages of Scripture and immortalized in the scarred hands, feet and side of Jesus. We know love not just because "the Bible tells me so," but also because we who follow Jesus have experienced His transforming love and mercy. We know love because the Spirit of Christ lives inside us and teaches us to know His love and give it away to a broken world. Because we know this love we are called to lay down our lives and live it out.

This broken world is blatantly before us: in the latest high-profile Hollywood divorce, celebrity suicide, local homicide, exploitation of children, international conflict, drought-induced famine or Western greed. God hears the cries and feels the pain. As Tim Keller says, Scripture shows us over and over that God is intensely concerned for the widow, orphan, immigrant and poor and if we don't possess that same burden, it's an indicator that something in our hearts is not right.

When we turn to God in the surrender of worship, our hearts can be made right. In worship, we regain a true and biblical perspective on the world we live in. Worship gives us a glimpse of kingdom life under the reign of Christ and calls us to live out the message of His Lordship for those who suffer under the reign of sin.

God's love is a generous love. His grace is abundant. We are to love because we have been loved. We can love because we have been loved.

Walking with God means doing justice, and doing justice is a way of life. It flows from an understanding of the grace we received and are commanded to give, out of the abundance in our hearts. Let your shout of love begin with even a whisper of His kindness. Let God's Spirit multiply your expressions of grace and mercy to the hearts of those He places in your path.

> There is a direct relationship between a person's grasp and experience of God's grace, and his or her heart for justice and the poor.
>
> *Tim Keller* [1]

Prayer: Lift it Up

Father, Your love is vast beyond our comprehension. That love is ours in Christ and has been freely poured out upon us. But forgive us, Lord, for our selfishness that hoards Your love. Forgive us for the fear that hides Your love from those who desperately need it. Though the need before us is overwhelmingly great, You, Lord, are enough for us and for all the sin and sorrow of the world. Thank You that we are filled with Your love and goodness. Enable us with the heart of compassion to live it out. Thank You that You have saved us, and that You've empowered us to bind up the broken. We seek Your mercy and justice in the lives of the broken and ask You to use us as Your agents of reconciliation. In Jesus' name. Amen.

For Discussion: Talk it Out

1. Read *Proverbs 11:24*. How does the act of giving make us richer? How does withholding make us impoverished?

2. As you read *Titus 3:3-7*, think back to life before Christ found you. What kind of brokenness were you experiencing apart from the grace of Christ? What part of the Gospel was the best good news to you?

3. Discuss Tim Keller's statement, "There is a direct relationship between a person's grasp and experience of God's grace, and his or her heart for justice and the poor."

Next Steps: Walk it Out

1. Start with simple, concrete expressions of giving. Pray for a hurting neighbor. Make a phone call to a lonely senior citizen. Buy groceries for a single mother.

2. Pray for a fresh revelation of the love of God. Ask Him to help you see how to live out His love.

3. Go before Jesus in prayer and offer your life to Him as a blank cheque. Surrender to Him your all, including your commitment to love and serve the poor in a life of worship and justice.

You are Good

You rescue the sinner
You walk with the weary
You carry the crippled
You are good
You comfort the broken
You lift up the needy
You stand upon justice
You are good

I will rejoice, I will rejoice in You
I will rejoice, lift my voice to You

You are good
You are good
And Your mercy lasts forever
You are good
You are good
And Your mercy lasts forever

Sean Dayton / Brent Milligan

You are Good

"Oh give thanks to the LORD, for he is good;
for his steadfast love endures forever!" – 1 Chronicles 16:34

Signposts

John Piper, in *Desiring God*, speaks of God's blessings as sunbeams. Drawing on a C.S. Lewis analogy, he describes how these blessings shine upon us, brighten our lives and encourage our hearts. But far beyond simple enjoyment, there is a greater purpose for these blessings. These rays of light invite us to walk into them and, in Piper's words, "see the sun from which they come. If the beams are beautiful, the sun is even more beautiful. God's aim is not that we merely admire his gifts, but, even more, his glory."[1]

The gifts of God, lavishly poured out on all who will receive, have been purchased at the cross and provided by grace. God loves to see us fully receive and enjoy these gifts, but, even more importantly, He desires that His gifts act as signposts, causing our eyes to look past the beams and marvel in new awareness of His glory and goodness.

Overwhelmed by Generosity

Have you been in that place recently where you've been overwhelmed with the blessings of God? Where you've been stopped in your tracks by His favor and unspeakable generosity? Whether it's gratitude for salvation, the joy of a spouse or a child, a home to live in, health, or the provision of food, we've all had the sunbeams of God's goodness shine upon us. The Psalmist David exclaimed, *"Oh, how abundant is your goodness, which you have stored up for those who fear you and worked for those who take refuge in you, in the sight of the children of mankind!" (Psalm 31:19)*

How do we respond to this generous God? How do we adequately answer this goodness and the heart from which it flows? We worship. Worship is our response to God, our love expressed in awe, adoration, and action.

Celebration of Mercy

Sean Dayton knows firsthand the rich goodness of God. He is a blessed man and a passionate worshipper. At church, late one night, with guitar in hand and alone with God, singing out of his grateful heart, he began to sing these words, "You are good, You are good, and Your mercy lasts forever." It was a simple chorus, but a deep response to the generosity of God. The rest of the song be-

> To be grateful is to recognize the Love of God in everything He has given us — and He has given us everything. Every breath we draw is a gift of His love, every moment of existence is a grace, for it brings with it immense graces from Him.
>
> Thomas Merton [2]

came an extension of those words as he reflected on God's heart for justice and mercy.

"You are Good" is, first of all, a celebration of the incredible mercy God extends to us. The verses joyfully recount God's rescue of sinners, the ultimate expression of undeserved grace. Further, the song tells of the God who walks with the weary and comforts the broken. The Bible declares that our God is One who *"raises the poor from the dust and lifts the needy from the ash heap." (Psalm 113:7)* Sean writes, "I can sing every line with conviction and sincerity because He has been those things for me." **There is power in a song when it originates in the Word of God, is born by the Spirit of God, and is sung from deep personal experience with God.**

> "What comes into our minds when we think about God is the most important thing about us. Worship is pure or base as the worshiper entertains high or low thoughts of God."
>
> A.W. Tozer [3]

Singing Leads to Doing

Worship leaders like Sean have the amazing privilege of leading songs that remind people of who God who is. Sean, like other worship leaders, recognizes that singing a song is not the end but just the beginning. Singing our worship leads us to demonstrate our worship through acts of showing mercy and doing justice. Sean's prayer is that, through this song, people would see God's lavish goodness and then desire to partner with Him in His pursuit of the lost and broken.

Our belief should determine our behavior. Our view of God should guide our actions. Our God is a God of goodness, justice and righteousness. *"Righteousness and justice are the foundation of your throne; steadfast love and faithfulness go before you." (Psalm 89:1)*

Sean's hope is that as believers understand more of God, they will approach their earthly relationships with His heart. He reflects, "When we realize that God cares about a person and loves them, we ask, 'How can I care for this person and love them?'" At the end of the day, all that we are and sing, say and do, is a response of love to Christ who sacrificed for us. All that we do is for His glory, the glory of the One who is good and whose mercy lasts forever.

Prayer: Lift it Up

    Father God, bottomless fountain of all good, giver of every good and perfect gift, we have received from Your hand countless blessings in Christ Jesus and we thank You. These are the great beams; Your glory is the radiant source. Help us to take nothing for granted but to be reawakened to the goodness from Your heart that loves us and has saved us. Receive our songs and renew in us the desire and courage to live these songs out as we love others in Jesus' name. In this we rejoice, that Christ has rescued us and given us the ministry of rescuing others in Your name. Amen.

For Discussion: Talk it Out

1. Have you found yourself overwhelmed with blessings of God? Stopped in your tracks by His favor and generosity?

2. Thomas Merton said, **"Gratitude therefore takes nothing for granted, is never unresponsive, is constantly awakening to new wonder and to praise of the goodness of God."** Why are we so often unresponsive to God's goodness and what can we do about this?[4]

3. "Our belief should determine our behavior. Our view of God should guide our actions. Our God is a God of goodness, justice and righteousness." What can you do to display God's goodness, justice, and righteousness in your own world, right now?

Next Steps: Walk it Out

1. Go to a quiet place, be still, and reflect on the goodness of God that has touched your life. Sing to Him a new song of gratitude, whether simple or profound, and offer out of your blessings that song of thanksgiving.

2. Make a list of five things you are deeply thankful for and determine to share your gratitude for one of these things with someone else today.

3. Make an inventory of five things you can live without and find some people who have need of those things. Bless them by giving them what you have been given.

4. Memorize Psalm 89:1: *"Righteousness and justice are the foundation of your throne; steadfast love and faithfulness go before you."*

FROM YOU FOR YOU

It's Your voice that called me from darkness
It's Your love that set me free
And every day You guide my way
And never ever leave

It's Your mercies new every morning
As You're overtaking me
So every day it's You I thank
For every good and perfect thing

But it's not all just for me
You wrote a bigger story
And the circle is complete
As I use what You give to bring You glory

You are my source, I know
It's your hand that feeds me
I am Your hand, to go
To someone who needs me
All that I have
All that I am take and use me
Teach me to give
Teach me to live in that beauty
'Cause everything I am
And everything I've got
It's from You for You from You for You God

It's my ransom fully paid
As I'm covered in Your shade
And anything that I could bring
It all came from You anyway

And the simple test of love
Do we do the things You said?
'Cause faith that doesn't move is dead

Dan Macaulay

3

From You for You

For from Him and through Him and to Him are all things.
To Him be the glory forever! Amen" – Romans 11:36

Knowledge + Action = A Life of Truth

We are on a journey together, discovering the truth of what the Lord requires of us and how we should live that truth out. **Being faithful in our
life of worship means that two essential concepts need to work together:
knowledge plus action, faith with works.** A.W. Tozer wrote, "For a long
time I have believed that truth, to be understood, must be lived; that Bible
doctrine is wholly ineffective until it has been digested and assimilated by
the total life."[1] God clearly spells out how He desires us to take "total life"
action in *Micah 6:8,* where He commands us to do justice, love kindness,
and walk humbly with Him. Our journey is one of growing to understand
the message of this verse more fully and to live it out more faithfully.

In the song, "From You for You," worship leader Dan Macaulay expresses his heart to go beyond simply having the knowledge of what's right, to living it out in action. Dan believes we are to use what we've been given

and love those around us with those gifts. His perspective is that worship is not about our personal enjoyment, but rather is about giving glory to God. As we place God at the centre of our lives and proclaim His Kingdom, we are also inviting others to enter into it.

Four Simple Words

Four words have helped Dan live in this reality: from You, for You. For Dan, this is a summation of what worship is all about. The phrase came to him a few years ago. Immediately he knew there was a song to be written. As he thought about the message and began to write the song, a number of Scripture passages filled his mind and shaped the lyrics.

First was *James 1:17*. For Dan, the essence of this song is that **God has handed us everything we have, and what we do with it in response is our worship to Him.** As grateful recipients, we thank Him, taking what He's given and using it for His glory. Next was *1 Corinthians 3:9*. In Christ, we are God's fellow workers, working in His field as He builds His Kingdom on earth. According to *1 Corinthians 10:31,* the gifts of grace He gives us are to be stewarded that He might be glorified. Finally, *1 John 4:19* came to him, with the message that worship is our whole-life response of love to Him who loved us first.

Sow and Reap

Dan has experienced the blessing of stewarding God's gifts, investing them into the Kingdom, and finding that God then gives us even more to work with. Dan has seen so clearly the fruit of the biblical principle of sowing and reaping *(Galatians. 6:7)* in his own life. He can recount specifically experiencing more grace as he obeyed God and put his faith in action. Those four words from You, for You, point to the passionate cry of Dan's heart. *"For from Him and through Him and to Him are all things. To Him be the glory forever! Amen" (Romans 11:36).*

In Dan's words, "By loving others, we're loving Jesus, because as much as we do it to them, we do it to Him *(Matthew 25:40).* We can't say we love God without also loving people created in His image *(1 John 4:20)*!"

For Dan, one of the most personally challenging concepts in the song is found in the words, "But it's not all just for me—You wrote a bigger story." Dan admits that it is easy to get caught up in selfishly building his own "mini kingdom." He says, "I need to be reminded to partner with God in building His Kingdom and trust Him to look after my family and the things we need, in that order" *(Matthew 6:33).* There is a bigger story and God invites us to be part of it, by using what we have for His global and eternal purposes.

Dan's hope is that this song will help believers understand these truths and motivate them to live boldly in the love of God. By putting a grand concept into a short catchy phrase he hoped that the message would stick in people's minds and engage their hearts. Dan is working on creating a website (www.fromyouforyou.com) where he will highlight what people are doing to serve others for the Lord's sake. He will be encouraging individuals and ministries to submit videos and stories about what they do to bring awareness about their work and encourage others to jump in and use what they've been given for God's glory. New ideas, off-the-wall ideas, and faith-stretching ideas can inspire us all to jump in and put our faith to work.

> "Obedience is the love language of the Almighty."
>
> Paul Carter [2]

Get it Going

The song's bridge puts the question directly to us: are we living out what we know? **"And the simple test of love, do we do the things you said? 'Cause faith that doesn't move is dead."** Dan sees the essence of worship clearly. "For me, boiling it all down, Jesus said: If you love me you'll keep my commandments. And if we say we believe, but don't act on it, then we don't really believe at all. So the evidence that we love Him and believe Him is our actions. And when we act on loving God by loving those created in His image, we complete the circle He intended all along."

Prayer: Lift it Up

Heavenly Father, we confess that we readily claim to love Your Word without doing the hard work of living it out. There is a cost to obedience and as Jesus did all You commanded, help us in this. Help us live what we believe, with Jesus Christ at the center of our lives. May we bring You glory as our desire to give motivates our hearts more and more. Help us shine our lights by involved action that others might see and glorify Your name. From You are all things and all the glory is Yours. Worthy God, we recommit ourselves to demonstrating our love for Your Word by believing and obeying it. We will, by Your grace, take our growing understanding of the biblical mission and add to it obedient biblical living. By the power of the Holy Spirit and in the name of our Lord Jesus Christ, we ask this. Amen.

For Discussion: Talk it Out

1. Discuss this statement by A.W. Tozer: "Truth cannot aid us until we become participators in it. We only possess what we experience."[3]

2. How, in your life, have you experienced the reality of the "sow – reap" principle?

3. What can be done to resist and destroy the predominant cultural idea that, "It's all about me!"?

4. What idea in this song and chapter most challenges you? Excites you?

Next Steps: Walk it Out

1. Ask God to reveal to you a truth you know that needs to be lived out to be fully experienced.

2. Put your faith into action by stepping out of your comfort zone and sharing the love of Christ in word and in deed. What will that look like?

   _____

   _____

3. "And the simple test of love, do we do the things you said? Cause faith that doesn't move is dead." Get moving on doing what you know you have been called by God to do to share your gifts and love of Christ with others.

Something to Give

Hey you, with the time why don't you spend it
If you've got a dime why don't you lend it
If you've got hands then get them reaching out
If you've got feet then get up off the couch

   There's nothing so rude
   As a gift you don't use
   Or a life that you choose not to live
   'Cause you're blessed to bless
   And the best of possessions is
   Having something to give

Hey you, with the song, why don't you sing it
If you've got a lunch why don't you bring it
And if you've got a dream don't let it die
If you've got a will come on and try

   There's nothing so rude
   As a gift you don't use
   Or a life that you choose not to live
   'Cause you're blessed to bless
   And the best of possessions is
   Having something to give

Strength that's wasted always wastes away
But love that's lived gets stronger every day

   There's nothing so rude
   As a gift you don't use
   Or a life that you choose not to live
   'Cause you're blessed to bless
   And the best of possessions is
   Having something ...
   You've got something to give

Carolyn Arends

4

Something to Give

The Lord said to him (Moses), "What is that in your hand?"
He said, "A staff." – Exodus 4:2

Blessed to Be a Blessing

Leading up to the writing of this song, Carolyn Arends had been re-flecting on God's covenant with Abram *(Genesis 12:2)* when He promised, *"And I will make of you a great nation, and I will bless you and make your name great, so that you will be a blessing."* She was convicted by the truth that when God blesses us, it is so that we can be a blessing to others. Beyond the blessing of receiving God's gifts is the deeper blessing of the joy of passing it on. Blessings that are merely stored up and kept for ourselves can quickly turn into curses, but given away, they bring life and joy.

She gives the example of Christmas morning to illustrate the point: Re-ceiving presents is a lot of fun, but giving presents can be even more fulfilling. When you find the perfect gift for someone you love, you can't wait for them to open it. The opportunity to give this gift and see the joy it brings the other person is so exciting. As simple as this example is, it underscores something profoundly important about the way God has made us. Carolyn says, "He's wired us for giving—or, more specifically—for being a part of what He is giving to His creation. **To have an opportunity to give our time, skills or resources is really an opportunity to be fully human, to live out the life for which we've been designed.**"

What's in Your Hand?

In *Exodus 3*, God declares that He has seen the affliction, heard the cries, and knows of the suffering of His people. He has compassion on them and He's sending deliverance from their oppression. The Lord chooses Moses and Aaron to be His instruments of mercy. Like many of us, Moses considers himself grossly inadequate for the task. He's a backwoods shepherd, with a royal upbringing and a fugitive past.

> Just a channel full of blessing
> To the thirsty hearts around
> To tell out Your full salvation
> All Your loving message sound
>
> Channels Only, Mary Maxwell [1]

When Moses objects, referencing his fears and weakness, God draws Moses' attention to what he does have, asking, "What is that in your hand?" Moses answers, "A staff," and God tells him to take that staff and lay it down before Him. This same staff will be powerfully used many times throughout the process of the Israelites' deliverance from Egypt.

When we stop and recognize all that we are, have, and know, we can see that our hands truly are full. We indeed have something to give, something that God can use to pour out His compassion upon those He loves. It is up to us to be good and wise stewards of His gifts.

The Adventure of Blessed Inclusion

The process of recognizing the gifts that are already in our hands, and learning to steward these gifts wisely and generously is an amazing adventure. Christ calls us to follow Him and imitate His life and ways. When He saw the crowds, Jesus had compassion for them because they were harassed and helpless, like sheep without a shepherd *(Matthew 9:36)*. Carolyn relates hearing someone say that **God subjects Himself to the indignity of relying on us to get things done (rather than just doing it all Himself) because He loves to include us in what He's doing.** She says she learns more and more what a privilege that inclusion is, and how essential it is to being truly alive. In her words, "I've realized that occasions to give—whether it's through child sponsorship, pitching in when a neighbour needs help, volunteering at our kid's school or rolling up our sleeves on a social justice project—need not be motivated by guilt but by a sense of opportunity and adventure."

God Uses a Song

A few years ago, Carolyn was in Japan and met a woman who had been a missionary there for 30 years. She told Carolyn she'd received her latest CD and that there was one song in particular that had really meant a lot to her and her husband. The woman explained that in the last year her husband had been stricken by a debilitating stroke and needed full nursing care while she was teaching at the missionary school. Carolyn was deeply moved that one of her songs had been a source of comfort to them. On that particular CD, there were a couple of songs about going

> But he said to me, "My grace is sufficient for you, for my power is made perfect in weakness." Therefore I will boast all the more gladly of my weaknesses, so that the power of Christ may rest upon me.
>
> 2 Corinthians 12:9

through valley times and Carolyn imagined it had to be one of those. But when she asked the missionary which song she meant, she told Carolyn it was "Something to Give", the most upbeat track on the CD! Carolyn actually thought she must have mixed up the titles. But there was no mistake, it really was that song!

As the two of them talked more, the woman expressed that, for her, the thesis of the song was: **if there is still air in your lungs, God still has something for you to do.** They were not going to give up or quit! She and her husband had clung to that truth, and as difficult as the last season of life had been, it had also been their most amazing time of ministry during their entire 30 years in Japan.

Upward and Outward

Carolyn loves N.T. Wright's conclusion from his reading of the biblical narrative: that humans are called to the twin vocations of priests and kings.[2] He describes how we are meant to stand at the interface between God and his creation. **In one direction, this means gathering up creation's praise and offering it to God (priestly worship). In the other direction, this means administering God's compassion and justice and mercy to His creation on His behalf (kingly stewardship).** Carolyn writes, "If we offer worship up to the Creator without being moved to carry His justice to His creation (or vice versa), we've truncated our calling and missed what He's made us for. If we sing praise to God but fail to '... *do justice and love mercy*' *(Micah 6:8)*, we betray the fact that we don't know our God (and what matters to Him) very well at

> *Through him then let us continually offer up a sacrifice of praise to God, that is, the fruit of lips that acknowledge his name. Do not neglect to do good and to share what you have, for such sacrifices are pleasing to God.*
>
> *Hebrews 13:15-16*

all." The call of the worshiper of God as priest and king is both upward and outward.

Something to Give

What's in your hand? What has God given you that you can give away? Is it a song? Sing it well. Is it time? Use it well. Is it money and resources? Spend them well. We are blessed, to bless. We have something to give. **His master said to him,** *"Well done, good and faithful servant. You have been faithful over a little; I will set you over much. Enter into the joy of your master." (Matthew 25:21)*

Prayer: Lift it Up

Gracious God and Heavenly Father, our lives overflow with Your good gifts. We are blessed to be a blessing. Help us to be those channels that reach out to share with others in need… whether in our churches, our community, or in other parts of the world. Use us to show your love that brings joy and salvation. Teach us the privilege and joy of giving what You have given us. In Jesus' name. Amen.

For Discussion: Talk it Out

1. Discuss this statement, "Blessings that are merely stored up, and kept for ourselves, can quickly turn into curses, but given away, they bring life and joy."

2. Tell about a time you experienced the great joy of giving the perfect present to someone you love.

3. What is biblical stewardship? How seriously do you think we should take it?

Next Steps: Walk it Out

1. How has God gifted you? Take inventory and list the gifts and talents you have. Think through how you can reach out to those in need with those gifts and talents.

   _____

   _____

2. Memorize *Matthew 25:21, "His master said to him, 'Well done, good and faithful servant. You have been faithful over a little; I will set you over much. Enter into the joy of your master.'"*

3. Pray and ask the Lord to show you someone who needs His love and mercy, extended through your life.

Defender of the Poor

Mike Janzen

To bless the poor with us
To feed the hungry ones

Is what You have taught us
To give as you have giv'n
To bring the orphans in

Is what You've commanded
Yet I am also poor in love
I need You, Lord, to fill me up

Defender of the poor
Restorer of the broken
Release for the oppressed
A shelter for the homeless
Is this not what it means
To know You, Lord of all
Is this not what's required to
Worship You above

To care for those in need
To set the captives free
To love as You showed us
To leave the harvest fields
For those without to eat
To tell of Your favour

5

Defender of the Poor

Righteousness and justice are the foundation of your throne; love and faithfulness go before you. – Psalm 89:14

An Awakening

It seems that, over the past few years, many Christian artists have been stirred by the Holy Spirit to begin thinking about and writing songs concerning the issue of worship and justice. A new awakening is happening. Believers dissatisfied with complacency have been opening their Bibles, finding out who God is and what He calls us to.

One man wakes, awakens another
Second one wakes his next door brother
Three awake can rouse a town
And turn the whole place upside down
Many awake will cause such a fuss
It finally awakes all of us
One man wakes with dawn in his eyes
Surely then it multiplies
Surely then it multiplies

The Great Awakening – Leeland [1]

When the news of this worship and justice compilation project got out, dozens of artists from across the country submitted songs. It was clear that there weren't just a few artists who were being moved by this issue, but many. **It seems that God is reawakening His Church to His heart and the missing pieces of our gospel.**

Overwhelmed by Mercy

One songwriter who was stirred was Mike Janzen. His song, "Defender of the Poor," emerged out of a desire to write a worship song that gathered together the overarching theme in the Bible of God and justice. Mike began by jumping into God's Word and gathered up all the Old and New Testament passages he could that talked about God's justice. The result was that he was overwhelmed by the magnitude of God's heart of mercy for the downtrodden and

> *He defended the cause of the poor and needy, and so all went well. Is that not what it means to know me?" declares the LORD.*
>
> *Jeremiah. 22:16 (NIV)*

the poor. He wrote down passage after passage until his journal was full of God's character and heart concerning the poor. As Mike reflected on passages like *Psalm 82:3-4*, he rediscovered that, at the centre of God's heart are the needy, oppressed, alienated, and downtrodden.

"Give justice to the weak and the fatherless; maintain the right of the afflicted and the destitute. Rescue the weak and the needy; deliver them from the hand of the wicked." (Psalm 82:3-4)

Having led worship for many years at his church's evening service, Mike had always wanted to write a worship song that spoke both of God's attributes and of those who are poor in this life. "Defender of the Poor" is that song; it tells of our God who defends the poor, restores the broken, brings release for the oppressed, gives shelter to the homeless, and then connects these actions of God with what worshipers are called to do in *Isaiah 58*.

"Is not this the fast that I choose:
    to loose the bonds of wickedness,
    to undo the straps of the yoke,
to let the oppressed go free,
    and to break every yoke?
⁷ Is it not to share your bread with the hungry
    and bring the homeless poor into your house;
when you see the naked, to cover him,
    and not to hide yourself from your own flesh?" (Is 58:6-7)

At the Front Door

Mike and his wife live in downtown Toronto and go to a church in the heart of the city. Obvious signs of brokenness are all around them. It is an area where those living with wealth and those living in poverty meet in a distinct contrast of super abundance and extreme need. Mike relates how, over the years, he and his wife have tried with some success and great failure to develop friendships with some of the people who live on the street and also with some of the new immigrants in the neighborhood.

Blessed are the poor in spirit, for theirs is the kingdom of heaven.

Matthew 5:3

As Mike wrote this song, he realized that the same heart of God that breaks for the materially poor in our world is the heart that also breaks for the spiritually desolate and poor. He also started to see a direct link between friends on the street and his own poverty of spirit. As Mike recounts, it was at that point when, "Suddenly the words of the song 'Yet I am also poor in love, I need You Lord to fill me up,' were true for me as well as for those on the margins of our society." As we minister to the poor and needy we are reminded of the grace we've received and the grace and mercy we continually need.

Do Something

If you are on the journey of trying to live like Jesus, you have experienced this struggle. We struggle with wanting to do the right thing. We struggle with knowing what to do. We struggle to do what will make a difference. We struggle to understand how the gospel in Word and the gospel in deed fit together. We may have more failures than successes. Mike shares a story about the complexity of trying to be like Christ in his relationship with a man we'll call Joe:

The church that Mike and his wife attend used to throw an event called Party in the Park. This event was put on for those in the neighborhood who would appreciate great food and good music. Some neighborhood professionals would show up but by far the biggest representation of people was from those who lived in nearby shelters or parks. Through the many years of doing this, Mike became good friends with Joe. Joe had been on the street for over 25 years. He would show up at every Party in the Park, grab a djembe, march up to the stage and begin playing with the band. At first this was shocking for the musicians and everyone watching, but after a few years Joe just became a part of the band. They all came to expect Joe to show up and were disappointed when he didn't.

Joe slowly became part of the fabric of the church and, from time to time, would show up at an evening service and then would need a ride home after the church service was over. Joe's "home" was a revolving door of alleyways, sewer grates, and abandoned corners. Mike recounts, "As I gave Joe a ride home, it broke my heart that he was out in the cold of winter while I was safe in my home. We did what we could to help him when his blankets went missing, but most of the time we felt completely helpless."

> You cannot be a follower of Jesus and not have a profound concern for the poor.
>
> Steve Bell [2]

The God Who is There

Beyond what we hope to do, or can do, God is always watching and working in mercy. As Mike puts it, "I find it deeply reassuring that long after I've gone to bed in the comfort of my warm home, there is a God who defends and watches over those who are out in the cold. I realize that, far past any good deed I can muster up, there is a Savior that constantly seeks the highest level of justice and completeness for those oppressed and forgotten."

"When I sing the chorus of the song," says Mike, "I remember the great love of God for those who have little or no voice in this world. **I remember that true worship involves all of my being and all of my resources.** I remember that to worship God is to love the poor and act on their behalf." Let the awakening grow. Let there be a new dawn in our eyes.

Prayer: Lift it Up

God of Justice and Defender of the Poor, we come to You, humbled by Your mercy. Awaken us, Lord. Give us Your heartbeat. We are poor in love and rich in possessions. We need courage to go and live out of the mercy we have received. Enable us to give justice to the weak and the fatherless. Help us maintain the right of the afflicted and the destitute. Summon us to rescue the weak and the needy. In Your power, deliver the oppressed from the hand of the wicked. When we are overwhelmed, remind us that You are at work. When we fail, lift us up to try again. When we succeed, may it be to Your glory. In all our attempts to live mercifully, may it point people to the Lord of mercy and His great salvation. Amen.

For Discussion: Talk it Out

1. What kind of worship and justice "awakening" are you seeing in your own life? In the church?

2. Is there a person like "Joe" the Lord has put in your life? How have you reached out? What have you learned?

3. Have you, like Mike, experienced the feeling of some success but great failure in your attempts to love the poor and needy? After reading this chapter how has your perception of success and failure changed?

Next Steps: Walk it Out

1. Grab your Bible and concordance and do a study of God's heart for the lost, poor and needy. You could begin with these passages: *Leviticus 19:9-18, Matthew 9:35-38, Luke 4:18-19, James 1:26-27.*

2. As a local church, have a carnival, music festival, BBQ or neighborhood party. Invite the neighbours to your property or take your party to where they are. Show love as you give, share, and get to know those around you.

3. Buy a blanket, sleeping bag, or warm jacket and ask the Lord who you can give it to as an act of compassion.

Light Of the World

I know that there will come a day
We're all together in that place
But until then we gotta get along
Divided we're weak, as one we're strong
So everybody grab a hand
A house divided cannot stand
We can't show His love until
We're a shining city on a hill

If we all just come together, let our hearts collide

Then maybe we'll find, that the Light of the world will shine
to the depths of the darkest night
That the Light of the world will shine through us
And maybe we'll see by our love that the world believes
and the captives will be set free
That the Light of the world will shine through us

We're the salt and we're the light
A blazing fire in the night
Burning for the world to see
Burning that they might believe
So let this fire in you burn bright
Wave the flag and join the fight
A revolution is at hand
Let's learn to love our fellow man

If we all just come together, let our hearts collide
If as brothers and as sisters, we would unify

Let it shine to the nations, let it cover the earth
Through our lips as we worship, and our hands as we serve

The Light of the world will shine
The Light of the world will shine
The Light of the world will shine
The Light of the world will shine

Starfield

6

Light of the World

"A new commandment I give to you, that you love one another: just as I have loved you, you also are to love one another. By this all people will know that you are my disciples, if you have love for one another." – John 13:34,35

A Glimpse Of Heaven

Many of us have had the experience of gathering with a large number of other believers and realizing the amazing joy of being part of the family of God. Maybe it was a men's or women's conference in a large open-air stadium, a regional youth camp, a national ministry conference for your denomination or a citywide prayer gathering. In that moment, you felt part of something much greater. You caught a glimpse of the glory of the Body of Christ coming together to truly worship together. Surely this is a glimpse of heaven.

Witnessing the Body of Christ unified in worship inspired the writing of this song. As a touring band for many years, Starfield has had the unique privilege of seeing believers from various backgrounds come together in worship. They have caught a glimpse of brothers and sisters, in different denominations and places in the world, united in worship. Their perspective allows them to dare to believe that, united together in love, believers will be a shining light to the dark world.

What If?

Jesus stepped into our darkness and declared, *"I am the light of the world"* *(John 8:12)*. Starfield's song, "Light of the World," asks the questions: "What would happen if God's call to believers to love one another was put into practice? What if the people of God, united in Jesus Christ, lived in the love of God, and lived it out? What impact would that have?"

The Bible is extremely clear when it comes to the subject of believers nurturing unity. Paul writes, *"May the God of endurance and encouragement grant you to live in such harmony with one another, in accord with Christ Jesus, that together you may with one voice glorify the God and Father of our Lord Jesus Christ" (Romans 15:5,6).*

The result of the unity that God desires and enables, by the work of the Spirit, is that with one voice we will glorify God as we love and serve each other and our communities. A Church unified in Christ is a shining light. When love and unity truly exist, people notice. From the place of unity we can fully extend the Gospel, as we demonstrate Christ's love and grace in action. The Apostle Paul instructs us on achieving this unified love:

Put on then, as God's chosen ones, holy and beloved, compassionate hearts, kindness, humility, meekness, and patience, bearing with one another and, if one has a complaint against another, forgiving each other; as the Lord has forgiven you, so you also must forgive. And above all these put on love, which binds everything together in perfect harmony. (Colossians 3:12-14)

A City That Shines

Jon Neufeld, writer of "Light of the World," says that the message of the song calls him to believe that we are God's plan for change in our communities. This call comes from Jesus: *"You are the light of the world. A city set on a hill cannot be hidden." (Matt. 5:14)* This is an extraordinary verse. Just as Jesus has declared in *John 8:12* that He is the light of the world, He also now bestows on His followers the same name. He invites us to join in His work of lighting the darkness. As the Church, we are the light of hope, and we are God's hands and feet to those desperate for that hope. This song is meant to call believers to set aside pride and differences within the Church, in order to unify around the common purpose of bringing Jesus, the Light of the world to all those living in darkness.

The lyric "a house divided cannot stand" most personally challenges Jon, as he grieves the fractures in the Church. In his words, "Where there is division, there is weakness and vulnerability." As the hearts of God's people "collide," Jon hopes to hear more stories of churches being unified in their desire to love the needy in their communities, and to communicate the truth of Jesus to them.

Selfless Action

Jon believes that worship has a missional aspect to it, that justice and compassion are a natural extension and the ultimate fulfillment of our worship. He says, "Worship should inspire us to go and to step out and give of ourselves to better the lives of others. Our worship response should always be to give, and to serve."

> We have realized that an artificial divide has been created between worship, evangelism and justice. This is a divide that has to end if we are to be a biblical people who obey God in all that we sing and say and do.
>
> Mike Pilavachi [1]

Moses reminds us that our time on this earth is short. He prays, *"So teach us to number our days that we may get a heart of wisdom (Psalm 90:12)."* While we live, we must live for what really matters. We have opportunity in this life to set aside our self-centered ambitions, to be truly compassionate and generous with our time, money, and energy. We are called to love one another and to *"do good to everyone, and especially to those who are of the household of faith" (Galatians 6:10).*

"Light of the World" calls for us to take action in service, without motive of what we could gain in return. Songs like this one are simple to sing, but tremendously more difficult to live out. Jon expresses the challenge of going against the grain of our natural desires of self-glorification in service. "I want to serve because I am commanded to, not because I need recognition or credit. God calls us to love without the expectation of reward." For each of us, the challenge is to sing the words and then back them up with selfless action. The more we give of ourselves to others, the more joy and fulfillment we will experience, and the "Light of the World" will truly shine through us.

Prayer: Lift it Up

Father God, You have brought us together as Your family, united in Jesus Christ. He is our light and salvation. Thank you for glimpses of heavenly glory, when we are worshiping together and we get a taste of what is to come in Your heavenly kingdom. Lord, we know that more need to hear of Your salvation and experience the touch of Your love and grace through us. Forgive us for how our witness is obscured by our divisions. Forgive us for our self-consumed lives. Father, unify Your Church. Teach us to number our days, and please give us courage to take action as we ask You to fill us up and send us out. Amen.

For Discussion: Talk it Out

1. Describe a time when you were in a place with other believers and you experienced unity in worship. What was it like?

2. How can you help grow unity in your fellowship, small group, or worship team?

3. Discuss this statement: "As the Church, we are the light of hope, and we are God's hands and feet to those desperate for that hope."

   Do you agree?

4. **Read** *Galatians 6:9-10, "And let us not grow weary of doing good, for in due season we will reap, if we do not give up. So then, as we have opportunity, let us do good to everyone, and especially to those who are of the household of faith."*

   What good can you do within your household of faith? What good can you do to someone who is outside of your faith community?

Next Steps: Walk it Out

1. Study the "one another" commands of the New Testament (e.g. see *John 13:35, Romans 12:10, Galatians 6:2, Ephesians 4:32*). Which one is your church strong in? Weak in?

2. Who in your fellowship can you partner with in an outreach to the needy of your community?

3. This week, find one person inside your community and one person outside your community and "do good" to them.

4. Each day this week, ask the Lord to fill you up and send you out, so your life can shine for Him.

REVIVE US AGAIN

Awaken our hearts Lord Jesus
Fill us again with Your fire
Stir up our zeal for You Lord
We need another revival
Give us a hunger to know You
A passion to seek Your face
Pour out a spirit of worship
On Your church again

Revive us again, Revive us again
Come renew Your works of power
Let Your Kingdom come
Revive us again, Revive us again
Come and rule our hearts Lord Jesus
Bring Your reign
Revive us again

Give us one heart, one vision
To finish the work You've begun
Move us with Your compassion
To reach out in mercy and love
Raise up Your church as an army
Your passionate holy bride
That with pure undivided devotion
We would lay down our lives

Andy Park

7

Revive us Again

Will you not revive us again, that your people may rejoice in you? Show us your steadfast love, O Lord, and grant us your salvation. – Psalm 85:6-7

Propelled

"In worship, God's truth presses in on us and propels us outward. For the worshipper there's a never-ending cycle of absorbing more of the love of God and a corresponding urge to spread that love around."[1] This vision has become Andy Park's heartbeat.

Andy is a music and worship ministry veteran. He came to faith in California during his university years and experienced the reality of the love of God and the power of the Holy Spirit. He prayed that the Lord would reveal more of Himself and he started to see the heart of God. His view of self, God and the world changed. He started asking, "What do you want me to do, God?" He experienced the overwhelming privilege of being loved by the King. Now many years later, and from the overflow of his walk with God, Andy has written hundreds of songs. He testifies that the songs come because God has captured his heart. God has revealed himself and Andy can't stop writing about it.[2]

Passion Lost?

As a music and worship ministry veteran, Andy experienced God's renewal of His Church in the 1980's and 1990's. Looking back to high points in his life and ministry over the last 25 years, he remembers a time when there was a greater desire and expectation for people to worship God and hear from Him. Andy is convinced we need God to stir us up again. In his words, **"Even the desire to seek Him is a gift from Him.** If we're not hungering to know Him and serve Him more, we need to ask for that passion."

> I counsel you to buy from me gold refined by fire, so that you may be rich, and white garments so that you may clothe yourself and the shame of your nakedness may not be seen, and salve to anoint your eyes, so that you may see.
>
> *Revelations 3:18*

It takes a lot of courage and humility to take an honest look at where we're at in our passion for Christ. Self-perception is easily skewed by self-deception. If we compare ourselves to others, we can always find reason to congratulate ourselves on how well we're doing. But the measure of our passion must always be a personal examining, asking Jesus to shine His light on what we're lacking, and to stir up our longing for Him as only He can. God loves to answer when we call on Him to revive us.

> Never be lacking in zeal, but keep your spiritual fervor, serving the Lord.
>
> *Romans 12:11 (NIV)*

Honest Examination

"Revive Us Again" is a passionate cry for the Lord to awaken His Church. Andy wrote this song as he considered passages like The Lord's Prayer and The Great Commission. He took an honest look and saw a lack of fire and zeal in the Church. He began to grow in his awareness that repeated renewal is necessary for the people of God, regardless of what generation they may live in. Throughout Scripture the people of God forgot Him. In mercy, God stirred them up, they called on Him for help and He answered them.

Andy says, "In asking God to 'let Your Kingdom come,' and 'bring Your reign,' we're asking for the Holy Spirit to fill us, rule over us and compel us to spread the generosity and good news of His kingdom." **That's what a renewal of the Spirit does; it compels us outward. Worship and mercy are inextricably intertwined.** A passion for God leads to a desire to show his compassion to the lost and needy.

Answered Prayer

Andy has personally sought the Spirit's renewal in his own life. He asked, "Give me your heart," and the Lord began to do it. Andy began to catch the connection between worship and mission. He recounts, "What I was experiencing was nothing new, but it was revolutionary." **Andy says, "God is not impressed with people who really know how to 'do church' but forget about securing justice for the poor.** As a worship songwriter, verses like these from the prophet Amos really get my attention: 'Away with the noise of your songs! I will not listen to the music of your harps. But let justice roll on like a river, righteousness like a never-failing stream!'" (*Amos 5:23,24, NIV*)

> Justice and mercy are intrinsic to God and therefore intrinsic to the worship of God.
>
> Mark Labberton [3]

Andy questions if we are too preoccupied with creating the best "worship show" while so much of the world is full of suffering. There's not a simple answer to that question. "Excellence in the arts doesn't necessarily preclude rivers of righteousness and justice flowing out from the church. **But the Church can make the mistake of catering to an entertainment-hungry society, labeling it as the worship that God desires, while forgetting about the foreigners, widows and orphans that are within a mile of the church's front doors."**

Worship in Action

Moved with God's compassion, Andy is living out his worship. In 2008, he and eleven other Christian artists gathered in Scotland to write songs for a CD project titled CompassionArt.[4] All the royalties from the CD and book were split between four CompassionArt sponsored projects and twelve artist-sponsored projects. CompassionArt is also the name of the charity that raises money to help breathe life into the poorest communities around the world, restoring hope and igniting justice.

> Evangelism means relationship. Find some people and love them, that will make a huge difference.
>
> Dave Toycen [5]

As a pastor, Andy and his congregation have gone out into the community to attempt to be Good News. They have put on free barbeques in low-income neighborhoods, reached out to addicts, supported refugees, handed out groceries to the needy, listened to people's stories and prayed for their struggles. It became very apparent that it made a huge difference for people to know that someone cared for them. Andy says, "Being a friend of God is the greatest privilege we could ever have. To worship Him means to extend that friendship to those around us, including the poor."[6] Simple friendship should be our primary means of reaching out to the needy all around us.[7]

The work of God through us begins with a work of God in us. What would happen if we had an undivided devotion and fervor for Jesus Christ? We would lay down our lives and understand that it's truly more blessed to give than to receive. We would, through simple acts of kindness, proclaim the worthiness of Jesus by emulating His life. Lord, will You not revive us again?

Prayer: Lift it Up

Awaken our hearts, Lord Jesus, fill us again with Your fire. Stir up our zeal for You Lord. We need another revival. Revive us again, revive us again. Give us one heart, one vision, to finish the work You've begun. Move us with Your compassion, to reach out in mercy and love. Revive us again, revive us again.

For Discussion: Talk it Out

1. Where do you need renewal and revival in your own life? Where does your church need renewal and revival?

2. How do you feel about asking for the Holy Spirit to fill you, rule over you and compel you to spread the generosity and good news of his Kingdom? Is that a prayer you are prepared to pray?

3. "Evangelism means relationship. Find some people and love them; that will make a huge difference." Tell about the person or people who found you and loved you and led you to Jesus. Are you willing to be that friend to someone God puts in your life?

Next Steps: Walk it Out

1. If you are an artist or have a band, put on a concert and raise money for the suffering church around the world, or a village riddled by drought and starvation.

2. Are there refugees in your community that need support integrating into culture? If so, be their friend, invite them to your home and give them assistance.

3. Pray this prayer: "Lord, wake me up with Your Spirit. Who can I help today?"

Break my Heart

I've longed for a vision
Could I only follow through
I'll miss Your great commission
To love just like You do
You've heard my prayers for wisdom
And You've heard me ask for strength
I need Your true conviction
Take my life in Your hands

Would You break my heart
With the things that break Your heart
Whoa, break my heart with that
Break the things that break Your heart
Break my heart

I seek no signs or wonders
I need no miracles
They're just a swirling dust trail
Behind everywhere you go
I'll be a light in darkness
And bring the hope of life
Is there a better reason
To do what I know is right

Stir in my being and shake out my soul
Courage to follow in truth that I know
To carry Your cross to wear Your name
O Lord this one thing I pray

Downhere

8

Break my Heart

If anyone would come after me, let him deny himself and take up his cross daily and follow me. For whoever would save his life will lose it, but whoever loses his life for my sake will save it. – Luke 9:23-24

Pray On

Prayer is powerfully transforming. Richard Foster writes, "To pray is to change. Prayer is the central avenue God uses to transform us."[1] Jason Germaine, of the band Downhere, was gripped by a prayer he calls "scary." It was Bob Pierce's prayer, "Let my heart be broken by the things that break the heart of God." Jason crafted the song out of his desire to explore with honesty the struggles to live out a life that follows after God. How often do we know what to do, yet don't do it? How often are we distracted by a substitute? How often do fleshly temptations drag us from the narrow way? Germaine writes what many of us experience, "I've longed for a vision, could I only follow through." Though we are often discouraged by our propensity to turn aside from following Jesus, we remember His words of encouragement. We don't give up praying. We press on.

Celebrity or Servant?

In our quest to be people who are "a light in darkness and bring the hope of life," Jason wrestles with the temptation we all face. Do we seek power or seek servanthood? The second verse contains these words, "I seek no signs or wonders, I need no miracles." Jason relates that phrase to the biblical account of Simon the Magician, who offered money to the Apostles so that he could have the power of the Spirit working through him, as they did.[2] The Apostle Peter responded, *"May your silver perish with you, because you thought you could obtain the gift of God with money! You have neither part nor lot in this matter, for your heart is not right before God"* (*Acts 8:20-21*).

Simon the Magician sought the things of God, yet for all the wrong reasons. He thirsted for prominence. He wanted to be in the center of the action. He was addicted to being a celebrity. Seeing the power of God, he wanted to obtain this power, leveraging it for his own selfish purposes. Our North American culture shares Simon's obsession to be noticed, in its blatant exaltation of the powerful and the popular. We see this all the time as those addicted to prominence and wealth elbow their way up the ladder of personal advancement and strategize for political advantage.

The Lure

Henri Nouwen tackles our temptation for prominence in his work, *In The Name of Jesus*. Wil Hernandez summarizes Nouwen's thoughts: "Even though many would consider relevance, popularity, and power as key ingredients of an effective ministry, they are, in reality, not vocations but temptations in the ministry. All three temptations lure us to return to the ways of the world of upward mobility and divert us from our mission to reveal Christ in the world."[3]

We want bigger, because our culture has told us bigger is better. We have believed the lie. God wants a heart that is right before Him. **We seek the brightness of the spotlight. God calls us to live in the shadow of the cross.** We seek to have our needs met. Jesus seeks servant leaders. "Who will follow Me?" asks Jesus. "Who will take up their cross and walk the narrow road with me?" Scripture compels us to see ministry through the lens of the life of Jesus. As Hernandez says, "The challenge for us is to tread the route of powerlessness, servanthood, and humility."[5]

> What makes the temptation of power so seemingly irresistible? Maybe it is that power offers an easy substitute for the hard task of love.
>
> Henri Nouwen [4]

We follow a crucified yet exalted Saviour. Jesus calls us to mourn, to be poor in spirit, to be meek, to die to self. Jesus' way is the epitome of counter-cultural. The narrow road is hardly mainstream and certainly not flashy. Are we willing to be obscure? Will we be faithful in serving, even if we get no applause?

May we not seek power, fame or control, but may we only desire to be followers of Jesus who are led to His heart, then led by Him daily, and led to introduce others to Him. May we live as humble servants to move in compassion and mercy into the dark and broken places of people's lives.

An Integrated Life

Just as Pierce's words gripped Jason's heart, his hope is that "Break My Heart" will become someone else's prayer and will be lived out, integrated into the ordinary moments of life. Seeing the Gospel integrated is hugely important to Germaine. **He knows that "social justice" is a trendy term and in some places it has become a diversion from an integrated Gospel of demonstration AND proclamation.** Actions of demonstration must be rooted and flow from the simple yet infinitely complex Gospel of Jesus Christ, who lived a sinless life, bore our suffering, died as our substitute on a cross, rose from the grave on the third day, and ascended to heaven. Jesus met physical needs but pressed in deeper to a person's heart with the call to repentance and to follow Him. Proclamation and demonstration work together, neither divorced from the other.

As we seek to be servants whose hearts are broken by the things that break God's heart, we will increasingly become those whose lives demonstrate the character of Christ lived out in both word and in deed.

Prayer: Lift it Up

Lord Jesus Christ, Maker of all things and Shaper of our hearts, change our hearts so that they will be better in tune with Your heart. Mold our hearts to long for the things You long for. Make us more like You so that we will intuitively do the same things You would do. Stir us and shake our souls. We need courage to follow You in the narrow way. Help us carry Your cross and wear Your name so that others will see and experience Your transforming forgiveness and grace. Amen.

For Discussion: Talk it Out

1. Discuss Richard Foster's statement, "To pray is to change."

2. Where do you wrestle with the temptation to be noticed?

3. How have the proclamation and demonstration of the Gospel been divorced from each other? How can they be integrated together in a way that is faithful to Jesus' call?

Next Steps: Walk it Out

1. Memorize *Luke 9:23-24: "If anyone would come after me, let him deny himself and take up his cross daily and follow me. For whoever would save his life will lose it, but whoever loses his life for my sake will save it."*

2. Offer hope to someone who has been forgotten: a shut-in person, a widow, a prisoner or someone who's marginalized. Bring both the words of the Gospel and the works of the Gospel to them.

3. Read Henri Nouwen's book *In The Name of Jesus.*

Jacob Moon

The voice crying out in the dark
Will never break down this wall
Or break my stony heart
If I don't answer that call

Coming from somewhere a million miles away from paradise
They prey on the young and they tell all kinds of lies
Like "We're just going for a little ride...it's gonna be ok
We'll be back before daylight..."

Hear me praying now, Lord

Can someone explain to me why nobody's standing guard?
I cover my ears and my eyes but reality hits back hard
As the money flies and the nations play their games
See the desperate eyes of the children bound and chained

The youngest of the young will be the first to go
They won't stop 'til they're done

Hear me prayin' now

Lord will You watch over the children of the world?
Cause it's a terrifying road now
      for the children of the world
Lord will You watch over the children of the world?
Cause it's a backbreaking load now for the
Children of the world

Child soldiers in the Sudan
They're training killers in Afghanistan
But whose war is it anyway?
We've seen enough unmarked graves
A generation of burned out slaves
But whose child is it anyway
Whose child is it anyway?

Hear me prayin' now

Lord will You watch over the children of the world?
Cause it's a terrifying road now
      for the children of the world
Lord will You watch over the children of the world?
Cause it's a backbreaking load now for the
Children of the world

Lord will You make us brave
To free the captive and the slaves
Lord bring Your justice to the
Children of the world

9

Children of the World

But Jesus said, "Let the little children come to Me, and
do not forbid them; for of such is the kingdom of heaven."
– Matthew 19:14

The Suffering Children

Stories from near and far tell of the neglect, abuse and exploitation of children. Many children in the West are left to raise themselves, "parented" by video games, screen time or gangs. Many children in the developing world are malnourished, orphaned, sold as slaves, or forced into human trafficking, child prostitution and soldiering.

According to Global Issues, **more than 26,500 children die each day due to preventable causes related to their poverty.**[1] Around 27 percent of all children in developing countries are estimated to be underweight or stunted. The two regions that account for the bulk of the deficit are South Asia and sub-Saharan Africa. About 72 million children of primary school age in the developing world were not in school in 2005; 57 percent of them were girls. Every year there are 350–500 million cases of malaria, with

1 million fatalities. Africa accounts for 90 percent of malarial deaths and African children account for over 80 percent of malaria victims world-wide.[2] International Justice Mission reports that nearly 2 million children are exploited in the commercial sex industry. The AIDS pandemic continues to rage, and the oppression of trafficking victims in the global sex trade contributes to the disease's spread.[3]

Embracing the Vulnerable

Against the backdrop of these realities, we remember that Jesus very intentionally welcomed children to come to Him, and He warned those who would hurt them. Children always need a defender. These words from Henri Nouwen call us to embrace those who are the most vulnerable and the most victimized… and who is more vulnerable than a child?

"Compassion asks us to go where it hurts, to enter into the places of pain, to share in brokenness, fear, confusion, and anguish. Compassion challenges us to cry out with those in misery, to mourn with those who are lonely, to weep with those in tears. Compassion requires us to be weak with the weak, vulnerable with the vulnerable, and powerless with the powerless. **Compassion means full immersion in the condition of being human."[4]**

Too Small to Ignore

Singer / songwriter Jacob Moon wrote "Children of the World," as a response to the reality of the abuse experienced by the young and vulnerable all around us. Jacob was struck by Jesus' stern warnings to any who would seek to bring harm to children. *Mark 9:42 says, "Whoever causes one of these little ones who believe in me to sin, it would be better for him if a great millstone were hung around his neck and he were thrown into the sea."* And Jesus made it beautifully clear that the kingdom of God belongs to those who come as little children.

Jacob was particularly inspired to write this song after reading Wess Stafford's book *Too Small to Ignore*. He was also impacted by his work with the International Justice Mission, an organization which seeks to bring freedom to the oppressed by rescuing children and families from sexual slavery. Jacob states: "The stats are shocking on just how many children in our world today languish in captivity, and we as Christians cannot stand idly by." **Having been exposed to the overwhelming need, his thought was, "What am I going to do with this information? It seemed like there was now a responsibility to act."** He likens this idea to a line in Sara Groves' song "I Saw What I Saw:"

I saw what I saw and I can't forget it.
I heard what I heard and I can't go back.
I know what I know and I can't deny it.

Learn to do good;
seek justice,
correct oppression;
bring justice to the fatherless,
plead the widow's cause.

Isaiah 1:17

The horrific images and scenes got stuck in Jacob's mind and disturbed his spirit until they finally came out in song and prayer. "That is really what 'Children of the World' is, a prayer for justice and restoration for those children who are trapped and voiceless. The song is a call to act justly and to love mercy," he says. Jacob has used this song at several fundraisers and church services where the focus has been on child trafficking or a broader theme of justice, and has heard from many that the song stirred them up to take action.

Worship That Extends

Jacob is certain that worship and compassion are inextricably linked. He says, **"God made it clear in *Isaiah 1:11-17* that He's not interested in worship just being about empty gestures, or confined to 'worship services,' but that it extends to learning to do good, seeking justice, cor-**

recting oppression, bringing justice to the fatherless and pleading the widow's cause."

This scripture reminds him that his work for justice as a songwriter and a human being is never done. He believes, "As it was once sung 'If one of us is chained, none of us are free.'" The challenge lies in keeping ourselves from falling into complacency or weariness. The challenge is to remember that the heart of God is for justice and if we truly love what He loves, it should show in what we do.

We are aware that children of the world are in great need. We have access to them and we have the ability to meet their needs. We can make a difference in the life of a suffering child, and as Jacob asks us, "Can someone explain to me why nobody's standing guard?" Jesus said, *"Whoever receives one such child in my name receives me, and whoever receives me, receives not me but him who sent me" (Mark 9:37).* Children are so incredibly close to the heart of God. Will we stand guard for them? Will we defend their cause?

Prayer: Lift it Up

Jesus, thank you that You love the little children of the world. Thank you that you are their great Defender. Lord, will you make us brave enough to face the cruel realties of the abuses that young lives all over the world face daily? Father, bring Your justice to the children of the world. Help us defend their cause as we lift our prayers, as we speak out against injustice, as we give our attention, time and money to make a difference and restore hope for these little ones. Bless those across the world who minister to vulnerable children: loving, feeding, rescuing, restoring, and teaching them. Give Your servants fresh strength for each day. Meet their needs by Your grace and use us to support them. As we serve the children of the world, we seek to serve You. Amen.

For Discussion: Talk it Out

1. What was your reaction to the statistics at the beginning of the chapter?

2. Reread the Nouwen quote. What part of that statement most deeply impacts you?

   "Compassion asks us to go where it hurts, to enter into the places of pain, to share in brokenness, fear, confusion, and anguish. Compassion challenges us to cry out with those in misery, to mourn with those who are lonely, to weep with those in tears. Compassion requires us to be weak with the weak, vulnerable with the vulnerable, and powerless with the powerless. Compassion means full immersion in the condition of being human."

3. Discuss what you have done to reach out and care for the children of the world. After reading this chapter, what are you compelled to do next?

Next Steps: Walk it Out

1. Are there children in your own local church that are fatherless or motherless? Living in poverty? As a family, reach out to these little ones in a practical way and show the love of Jesus.

2. Plan to travel to a developing country to minister to children bound in hopelessness and poverty.

3. Investigate ways to give to ministries working to alleviate malaria and malnutrition in the most needy parts of Africa and Asia.

REAL LIFE OFFERING

So much more than a song we sing
So much more than a Sunday fling
You want us all to answer Your call
Give it all

So much more than the words we say
So much more than an hour a day
You want our lives to boldly exclaim
That God is real today

You want food for the hungry
Love for the lonely
Justice and mercy for those treated poorly
Tears for the lost and wounds from our cross
This is the worship you seek
A real life offering

Precious Lord, would you change our hearts
Light a spark so a fire can start
Showing how precious holy lives are
Change us to want

Food for the hungry....

So much more than just a song
So much more than just our words
For You long to see us bring
A real life offering

Brad Guldemond

Isaiah 58:6-12

6 "Is not this the fast that I choose:
    to loose the bonds of wickedness, to undo the straps of
the yoke,
    to let the oppressed go free, and to break every yoke?
7 Is it not to share your bread with the hungry
    and bring the homeless poor into your house;
when you see the naked, to cover him,
    and not to hide yourself from your own flesh?
8 Then shall your light break forth like the dawn,
    and your healing shall spring up speedily;
your righteousness shall go before you;
    the glory of the Lord shall be your rear guard.
9 Then you shall call, and the Lord will answer;
    you shall cry, and he will say, 'Here I am.'
If you take away the yoke from your midst,
    the pointing of the finger, and speaking wickedness,
10 if you pour yourself out for the hungry
    and satisfy the desire of the afflicted,
then shall your light rise in the darkness
    and your gloom be as the noonday.
11 And the Lord will guide you continually
    and satisfy your desire in scorched places
    and make your bones strong;
and you shall be like a watered garden,
    like a spring of water,
    whose waters do not fail.
12 And your ancient ruins shall be rebuilt;
    you shall raise up the foundations of many generations;
you shall be called the repairer of the breach,
    the restorer of streets to dwell in.

10

Real Life Offering

Jesus taught, "Whoever has my commands and keeps them is the one who loves me." – John 14:21

Worship as Obedience

As we grow in our spiritual maturity, we go beyond simple expressions of verbalized love and move to deeper and more sacrificial expressions. One way of growing deeper as a worshipper of Christ is by understanding the concept of worship as obedience.

Singing a song is easy. Living out the song in a life of obedience is the challenge. This life of obedience is the path of those who would follow Jesus. The more we progress in living obediently to Jesus' commands, the more authentic our love becomes, and the more glory we bring to God. Why is this essential to our discipleship? Simply because the Church exists for God's glory. All that we say and do is meant to bring glory to God (*1 Cor. 10:31*).

More Than a Song

The song "Real Life Offering" moves us deeper into our worship life by confronting us with the questions: what is the worship God seeks, and what brings glory to God? We know we are to worship by singing praise to God—the Psalms call on believers to sing 67 times (in the ESV Bible). But it is far more than a song God wants. **We are to worship Him by a life that proclaims and demonstrates who He is.** *Paul writes in 1 Corinthians 10:31 , So, whether you eat or drink, or whatever you do, do all to the glory of God.*

Brad Guldemond wrote "Real Life Offering" during his Bible college years. One day, after reading *Isaiah 58,* he sat down at the piano and this chorus began to emerge:

> You want food for the hungry love for the lonely
> Justice and mercy for those treated poorly
> Tears for the lost and wounds from our cross
> This is the worship you seek
> A real life offering

Worship That is Expressed in Compassion

Brad recalls his reflections on *Isaiah 58:* "Israel was doing what they thought pleased God, yet God said that what they were doing was not what He was looking for. They thought their fasting, studying, and worshipping would please God. But they weren't doing it out of a heart of love; they were doing it for themselves." Brad realized that without the proof of a life of kindness and compassion, worship is empty.

God is after worship that extends to addressing injustice, lifting burdens off the oppressed, sharing food with the hungry, and providing the homeless with shelter.

These convictions unsettled Brad, who found himself removed from the realities of a broken world. Like many believers, Brad grew up immersed in Christian culture (Christian elementary school, Christian summer camps, Bible college). For those who have had a Christian upbringing, it is easy to become isolated, saturated, comfortable and complacent. Brad became increasingly aware that much of his spiritual experience was focused only inward. His worship was isolated from the rest of his life—an hour on Sunday, and a daily devotional time. For Brad and for many of us, worship can easily become just about "me and God," without translating outward in our living.

Pour In, Pour Out

Personal and corporate worship times are essential to building a deep and mature Christian life, but these times are meant to fill the believer so that God's goodness and healing grace can overflow from us into the lives of others: the lives of those who need food, need a friend, and need to experience the love of God in action through us. God does not want just a part of us; He wants our whole life. He doesn't want us to simply consume "worship experiences" for our benefit. God wants to pour into us, so that we can pour into others. We are to give out of our abundance, loving the poor and caring for the needy.

> God is not impressed with fastidious religious observance when the daily lives of his people are filled with wickedness. God says in effect, "Your fasting and sackcloth are meaningless to me so long as you continue in rank disobedience to more important commands."
>
> Kevin Deyoung and Greg Gilbert [1]

Many worshippers seek to go beyond a "good worship" experience and offer "great worship." The concept of "great worship," however, needs to be redefined. True worship, the worship God seeks, loves God and those He loves. True worship is reaching out beyond ourselves and our walls, sharing what we have with the poor, caring for the homeless, and loving those who are hurting. *James 1:27 teaches, "Pure and undefiled religion before God and the Father is this: to visit orphans and widows in their trouble, and to keep oneself unspotted from the world."*

Authentic Worship

As we live out our worship and love of God in expressions of kindness and mercy to our world, it will radically transform our corporate worship experience. When individual believers live a lifestyle of obedience to Jesus' commands, corporate worship comes from a deeper and more authentic place. As we reach out to those in need, **we meet Jesus in the broken places. There, we are reminded of the extravagant grace that has reached out to us in our brokenness.** "Great worship," then, arises out of gratitude for God's mercy in our poverty of spirit and our privilege to share that mercy with others.

Jesus said, *"Let your light shine before others, so that they may see your good works and give glory to your Father who is in heaven" (Matt. 5:16, ESV).* From a passionate heart of worship comes a shining light that radiates the presence of Christ and shows itself in good works. Together, proclamation and demonstration become a real life offering to God.

The worship God seeks from us is to follow after Jesus in the way of obedience. This is clearly something we cannot do in our own strength. If we seek to walk in deeper expressions of worship through obedience, we will need the powerful and transforming work of the Holy Spirit to change our hearts. This is the path God has each one of us on. In love for Him and those He loves, let's follow where He leads.

Prayer: Lift it Up

Worthy God, all glory to Your name, who loved us in our poverty and lifted us out of the pit of despair. Forgive us, Lord, for a worship that focuses inward and fails to extend to others. Forgive us for thinking that a song is all You require, and not a life that backs up the song. Please change our hearts and transform our thinking so that grateful expressions of praise and obedient demonstrations of compassion might be the offering we bring for Your glory. Move us to action to love those You love. In Jesus' name we pray. Amen.

For Discussion: Talk it Out

1. Have you experienced isolation from the reality of the brokenness of the world due to immersion in Christian culture?

2. How is worship through demonstration a "greater" expression of worship?

3. Discuss this statement: "As we live out our worship and love of God in expressions of kindness and mercy to our world, it will radically transform our corporate worship experience."

---

4. What idea from this chapter or song lyric has impacted you the most?

Next Steps: Walk it Out

1. Take a friend or your family and volunteer in a food bank or shelter, deliver groceries to widows, or feed the homeless.

2. If you are part of a worship team, take your team and perform your music in a place where God's light is needed. Sing and minister in a nursing home, hospital, prison, group home, youth centre, or a downtown park.

3. Is there someone in your life who is lonely? Going through a divorce? Experiencing grief due to loss? What can you do to reach out to them with kindness?

4. Ask God for a way to demonstrate His love. Ask for strength to put your worship into action.

Least of These

Theres a little boy crying for something more to eat,
He is hungry. No one sees.
In a darkened room feeling like her bodys not her own,
She is dying, all alone.

Theres an orphan girl weakened from the heat of the day,
She is thirsty, and afraid.
And a stranger walks along this lonely, broken road,
Says life is hard but no one knows.

Does anyone see? Does anyone care?
Does anyone know theyre not alone? Im right there.

Whatever you've done for the least of these,
You have done for Me.
Can you see Me in her face,
Or in his hands and feet?
Whatever you've done for the least of these,
You have done for Me.
Take off your rose colored glasses
And see what I see.

Theres a younger man who cant forgive himself for what he's done,
Behind prison bars, got no one.
And shes living in the streets on the ground tonight,
With no place to go, its cold outside.

Does anyone see? Does anyone care?
Does anyone know theyre not alone? Im right there.

I was hungry, I was thirsty
I was on the street last night.
And I was dying, I was lonely,
Im in prison, cant you see,
That all along it was Me?

It was Me.
Whatever youve done for the least of these,
It was for Me.
Yeah, for Me.

Jill Hagen

11

Least of These

And the King will answer them, 'Truly, I say to you, as you did it to one of the least of these my brothers, you did it to me.'
– Matthew 25:40

Eyes of Compassion

Does anyone see? Does anyone care? These are the haunting questions that come from the voice of Jesus in Jill Hagen's song, "Least of These." Sure, we see many things, but do we see as God sees? Do we care as He cares? The lyrics of the song invite us to see hungry children, sex-trade workers, orphans, homeless people, the lost, lonely, and the imprisoned as those Jesus deeply cares about. This song invites us to act out of His compassion. Those described in this song are in the far-off places of the world, yes, but they are also in our communities, all around us, every day. Do we see? Do we care?

Matthew writes about Jesus: "When he saw the crowds, he had compassion for them, because they were harassed and helpless, like sheep without a shepherd. Then he said to his disciples, *"The harvest is plentiful, but the laborers are few; therefore pray earnestly to the Lord of the harvest to send out laborers into his harvest"* (Matthew 9:36-38).

David Ruis says, "As followers of Jesus, we cannot ignore what moved Him to send out the first of His disciples, what moves Him still to send us out today: compassion."[1] Jesus wants His followers to see how He sees, feel what He feels and go with His compassion as laborers in his harvest.

Overwhelmed

Singer / songwriter Jill Hagen describes how she was exposed to the needs of starving children from World Vision's TV programs. As she saw the desperate plight of thousands of starving children, she admits, "It was so hard to watch that I often would turn the channel." Jill was overwhelmed by the massive needs of the suffering children around the world. She felt like she couldn't make a difference, so why even try? How many of us have done the same thing when seeing things we didn't know how to deal with?

The First Steps

Several years passed and she decided to become a World Vision child sponsor, thinking it was a good first step. She was given a 4-year-old boy from Kenya, named Chrispian. That summer she had made plans to go on a mission trip to Kenya and was excited by the possibility that she might get to meet her sponsor child. She and eleven other Canadians went to Africa, praying that God would use them to love those God loves. A few team members from World Vision arranged to pick Jill up from the village her team was in and took her two hours north to meet her sponsor child. When she arrived in Chrispian's village, he was playing in the schoolyard. It was an unbelievable experience for Jill. She recalls, "The little boy that I had seen only on a picture card was real!"

Chrispian lived with his mother, twin brother and sister in a small mud hut. Jill sat down under a canopy with the family, drinking chai tea with them and giving the gifts she'd brought for Chrispian. That afternoon, she got to witness, up close, the amazing things that World Vision had been able to do to help the community become self-sustaining and she got to meet a family who was benefiting from her support, specifically. The whole experience of the mission trip and visit to Chrispian allowed Jill to see just a little bit of God's heart for the poor. In Africa, God spoke to her, gently: "Whatever you've done for the least of these, you have done it for me."

Changing

When she returned to Canada, Jill felt unsettled. The people she had shared a few short moments with in Kenya had so little material wealth but had so much joy. After reading *Matthew 25:31-46* she started to realize that helping the poor did more than benefitting them, the giving was also changing her. She came to understand that being around those in need helped her see more of Jesus' love for the poor and outcast. Jill realized that the needy weren't just in Africa, but all over her city. She didn't have to go far to find them.

Justice, "is not an activity as much as it is an attribute and aspect of character to be developed. A way of living. A way of seeing."

David Ruis [2]

Two months after returning from the mission trip she wrote "Least of These." She wanted to capture a piece of Jesus' heart for the broken and poor. She wanted to challenge her listeners and herself to see the world as God sees it, without "rose-colored glasses." God has been using this song powerfully in many people's lives as Jill sings it throughout North America. She has received many responses from those convicted by the lyrics and several have gone on to sponsor children.

Kenya changed Jill. She says, "Though I desire to see Jesus in each of the least of these, I sometimes struggle to see beyond myself. **I realize I too am the least of these.**" Overwhelmed by God's grace to send Jesus to die for her, she wants her entire life to be about the worship of God as she serves others. "The real challenge," she admits, "is walking in simple obedience everyday; to live out God's call to the needy, to visit someone in the hospital, talk with a homeless man on the street or sing for the youth that are "trouble" to society. I pray that God continues to break my heart for the very things that break His."

Prayer: Lift it Up

Lord Jesus, Saviour of the least, thank You that in Your compassion You reached out to us in our lost state, finding us in our place of poverty and rescuing us. We repent of turning away and choosing not to see. We confess our struggle to see beyond ourselves. We confess our blindness. We confess we have often not heard Your voice or responded to Your call to live with compassion. Give us eyes to see, a heart to feel, and the will to act. Give us the privilege of making a difference in Your name, one need and one person at a time, for Your glory. Amen.

For Discussion: Talk it Out

1. Describe a time when you saw, but didn't see, or when you saw but looked away because the truth was inconvenient and hard to process?

2. Who are the least in your world? Your church? Your city? Who is most easily forgotten about?

3. Discuss David Ruis' statement, that justice "is not an activity as much as it is an attribute and aspect of character to be developed. A way of living. A way of seeing." How is justice developed? How is it a way of seeing? How can you make it a way of living?

Next Steps: Walk it Out

1. "The harvest is plentiful, but the laborers are few; therefore pray earnestly to the Lord of the harvest to send out laborers into his harvest." Pray that the Lord of the harvest helps you see as He sees, care as He cares and sends you to act as He would act.

2. Speak with your pastor about the unmet and overlooked needs in your local church and community. What can you do to be involved?

3. Become a child sponsor and make the difference in the life of a child in a needy country.

Break God's Heart

Ali Matthews

One ordinary moment
losing this foolish pride
humbled for even just a moment
chasing my selfishness aside

Could I bring a simple kind of offering
Could I make a difference to this day
Enter in the heartaches of the suffering
And sing with the sorrows of the slaves
For I have eyes to see
And I have ears to hear

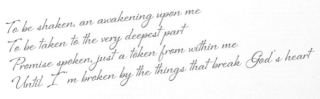

To be shaken, an awakening upon me
To be taken to the very deepest part
Promise spoken, just a token from within me
Until I'm broken by the things that break God's heart

Sinking in muddy water
No one could even see their pain
Heaven cries for all our sons and daughters
Every tear is a drop of rain

Could I bring a simple kind of offering
Could I make a difference to this day
Enter in the heartaches of the suffering
And sing with the sorrows of the slaves
For I have eyes to see
And I have ears to hear

River flow inside me
Holy tears of the Almighty

One ordinary moment
losing this foolish pride

12

Break God's Heart

"The Spirit of the Lord is upon me, because he has anointed me to proclaim good news to the poor." – Luke 4:18

One Week with Jesus

What would it have been like if you could have spent one week with Jesus? What would you have seen? Where would you have traveled? What would you have experienced? What miracles would you have witnessed? Imagine getting to see Him touching lepers, forgiving women caught in sexual sin, restoring hope to grieving parents, healing blind eyes, telling stories to children while he held them on His knee, and weeping for a close friend who had died. Jesus preached, taught, instructed, rebuked, healed, defied natural laws, and amazed all who heard Him. In all He did, His life was a testimony to the heart of God.

Jesus responded to human suffering with deep emotion: compassion, sadness, and grief over the effects of sin upon the lives of God's image bearers. He was broken over this broken world. At the outset of His ministry, Jesus announced His call and His mission saying:

"The Spirit of the Lord is upon me, because he has anointed me to proclaim good news to the poor. He has sent me to proclaim liberty to the captives and recovering of sight to the blind, to set at liberty those who are oppressed, to proclaim the year of the Lord's favor." (Luke 4:18,19)

The Pursuit of Brokenness

Ali Matthews grew up facing the needs of the broken. Her father, Lennox Brown, was a man of God with a great heart of compassion. As a scholar, preacher, and respected lawyer, he worked on the Board of Directors and as a lawyer for World Vision Canada for over two decades. She recalls a conversation she and her father once had about happiness. He pointed out that the world endorses the pursuit of happiness as the ultimate goal of life, yet Jesus modeled a life that was not particularly "happy." Jesus was a man with a heavy heart. Her father said that perhaps Jesus was showing us that our greater purpose is not to pursue happiness but to pursue love and compassion with a depth of conviction that will truly break our hearts.

> *Therefore be imitators of God, as beloved children. And walk in love, as Christ loved us and gave himself up for us, a fragrant offering and sacrifice to God.*
>
> Ephesians. 5:1-2

The World Shaking

In the early months of 2010, Ali was writing songs for her next CD project but her efforts kept being interrupted, as she says, "by global heartbreak." The world seemed to be falling apart with one disaster after another. She watched in shock and horror as Haiti crumbled to pieces following a devastating earthquake. Then came the floods in Pakistan. There were heat waves, subsequent forest fires, more floods, avalanches and hurricanes, all around the world. The list seemed to go on and on, leaving a trail of death, suffering and homelessness.

As a songwriter, she felt challenged to respond to all this global sorrow but often found herself at a loss. "What does He want us to do? How does he expect us to respond?" Ali was gripped by these questions. She then remembered a quote she had heard from World Vision founder, Bob Pierce. While traveling the globe as an evangelist in the 1940's he encountered widespread poverty. Pierce was moved with compassion and wrote these words in the flyleaf of his Bible, "Let my heart be broken with the things that break the heart of God." He began educating North American churches about the poverty he had seen and started raising money to help suffering children. In 1950, he incorporated this personal mission as World Vision.

> The LORD is near to the brokenhearted and saves the crushed in spirit.
>
> Psalm 34:18

The Heart Breaking

Ali responded to the global calamities by writing "Break God's Heart." This song was composed as a challenge to herself to respond to suffering with deep compassion and action. Ali's constant prayer is that she might be shaken out of her comfort zone and truly love people as Christ commanded us. She confesses that she wants to be the person this song is talking about, but "my own selfishness and fear often keep me in safe places and out of God's will." She also describes how, "Sometimes it's easy to speak the words of love and hope and still not feel heartbroken enough to respond with any kind of sacrificial action." The song lyrics underscore this: "Promise spoken, just a token from within me, until I'm broken."

Invited to Share in His Suffering

God's love for His creation is a powerful mystery. As Ali explored the thought of God's heart being broken, she struggled to grasp why an all-powerful, perfect God would even bother to feel grief for his fallen creation. She always thought it was odd that Jesus wept at the tomb of his friend Lazarus, for, as God, He would have known that He was about to raise Lazarus from the dead. She asks, **"So why did Jesus weep? I wonder if He was showing us that the heart of God can indeed be broken?"**

Will the things that break God's heart break ours as well? It is not just enough to know that God feels pain when his children suffer. The Man of Sorrows invites us to share His heart, to share in His suffering. As followers of Christ, we need to be

> *Yet it was the will of the Lord to crush him; he has put him to grief;*
>
> Isaiah 53:10

shaken, awakened, and taken to the very deepest part. This song reminds us to step outside of our selfish desires and enter into the heartache of the suffering.

Prayer: Lift it Up

Lord Jesus Christ, You are the Friend of Sinners and Healer of the Broken. Called to redeem a world under the effects of sin, in humility You were broken for us. Suffering Servant, surely You have borne our griefs and carried our sorrows. We are in awe of a God with such a mysterious heart of love and compassion. Help us to be like You, Lord—to be filled with that same compassion. Give us Your heart and break our heart with what breaks Yours. Amen.

For Discussion: Talk it Out

1. If you could have spent one day with Jesus, what would you have wanted to see and experience? What part of Jesus' heart do you think that would have revealed to you?

2. Many seek the pursuit of happiness as their ultimate goal. What's yours? How does this correspond to the mission of Jesus?

3. What news event—local, national, or global—has recently caught your attention and gripped your heart? What does it reveal about the brokenness of our world?

Next Steps: Walk it Out

1. Where in life have you been broken? In authenticity and transparency, share your story with someone and celebrate the healing power of Jesus Christ.

2. Memorize and meditate on *Isaiah 53:3-4,*

   "He was despised and rejected by men;
   a man of sorrows, and acquainted with grief;
   and as one from whom men hide their faces
   he was despised, and we esteemed him not.
   Surely he has borne our griefs
   and carried our sorrows;
   yet we esteemed him stricken,
   smitten by God, and afflicted."

3. Read the newspaper or listen to the radio. As you are exposed to heartbreaking stories or events, pray for God's mercy to flow into those situations.

4. Read through one of the gospels. As you study the life of Jesus and read of His compassion, pray that your heart might be broken with the things that break the heart of God.

THE ADVENTURE OF JESUS

Kevin Boese / Brian Doerksen

I want to live the adventure
I want to burn with the passion
I want to be filled with the presence of Jesus
I want to pray with the power
I want serve with the kindness
I want to live the adventure of Jesus

Blessing the poor, healing the sick
This is the life of love that Jesus lived
Teaching the heart, forgiving the sin
This is the life of love that Jesus lived

Then He said, we would do these very things
Here and now, I want to find out what that means

Blessing the poor, healing the sick
This is the life of love I want to live
Teaching the heart, forgiving the sin
This is the life of love I want to live

All I need, is to give what I have
Here and now, I want to see the Kingdom come

13

The Adventure of Jesus

Do not be slothful in zeal, be fervent in spirit, serve the Lord.
– Romans 12:11

Fully Alive

"I want to be fully alive. I want to fully embrace what God intends for me." These are words of one who has had the spiritual embers of his life stirred up. Kevin Boese wrote "The Adventure of Jesus" out of his discontent with his own complacency. The Spirit of God lives in us, but a contented self-satisfaction often grips believer's hearts and distracts them from the things of God. The Bible is clear that complacency is a real and present threat. We are told that because of sin, the love of many will grow cold.[1] We are warned in *1 Thessalonians 5:6, "So then let us not sleep, as others do, but let us keep awake and be sober."* While our natural tendency is to fall asleep spiritually, God wants us to be fully alert and moving forward in our worship walk.

If you have been a believer for any length of time you know that following Jesus is an adventure: it's exciting, daring, risky and unpredictable.

The Apostle Paul lived this adventure all across Asia and into Europe. He was no stranger to faith, risk or suffering. He wrote that Christians should not be lagging in diligence but, *"fervent in spirit, serving the Lord." (Romans 12:11)* He called believers to be *"steadfast, immovable, always abounding in the work of the Lord," knowing that in the Lord their labor is not "in vain." (1 Corinthians 15:58)* Life lived with Him, for Him, and by His power, is the most exciting experience possible on earth. This song calls us to walk with Jesus in the adventure of faith.

> Blessing the poor, healing the sick, this is the life of love that Jesus lived.
>
> *Kevin Boese and Brian Doerksen [2]*

The Adventure of Writing a Song

When he began writing "The Adventure of Jesus," Kevin was part of planning an interdenominational, citywide event called "Love Abbotsford," The focus of this outreach was for multiple churches to engage in various acts of kindness on a particular Saturday in June. Following the day of service, the churches would all gather in the evening for a worship celebration.

The local area leaders decided to do a live recording of the Love Abbotsford worship time and Kevin was hoping his new song would fit into the set. The problem was that the song wasn't ready yet. He liked the chorus of the song, but wasn't satisfied with the verses. Fellow worship leader Brian Doerksen heard the song and felt the same way. He encouraged Kevin to keep working at the song to create stronger verses. Kevin tried some different versions, but still was unhappy with the verses. When he felt he'd exhausted his creative ideas, Kevin asked Brian if he would co-write with him and Brian said yes.

Kevin remembers driving to Brian's house for their first session on the song, feeling so honoured that his friend, an accomplished recording artist, would partner with him in the process. Together, they started working on a couple of ideas but they didn't really get anywhere. Kevin's heart sank as Brian put down his guitar and suggested that they should move on to something else for a while. But then Brian paused, grabbed his guitar again, and said, "Here's an idea…blessing the poor, healing the sick…" and started playing the first line of the song, pretty close to how it is now in its finished state. The song quickly took shape and the possibility of it being used for the June event excited them both. The pair emailed a few more lyrical ideas back and forth over the next couple of weeks and then were able to finalize it. The anthemic song was used for that June event and included in the live recording.

Live the Truest Adventure

For Kevin, while his life definitely isn't a daily "wild and crazy adventure," as he looks back at the various steps of faith he and his wife Nancy have taken, it does feel like he's been on an adventure with Jesus. Kevin says, "Even the most 'normal' life can be an adventure with Him! God has a way of shaking us up by taking us out of the familiar and comfortable into something different."

And Peter answered him, "Lord, if it is you, command me to come to you on the water." He said, "Come."

Matthew 14:28-29

Kevin says, "This song continues to challenge my propensity for complacency while reminding me that it is the presence of Jesus in me that is life. "Worship," says Kevin, "isn't really worship if it's not reflecting a life of worship; truly loving God, others, and ourselves. The great commandment is not just concerned with the vertical, but also with the horizontal." The song reminds us that we are meant to physically and spiritually do the things Jesus did in his time on Earth. We are to give what we have and see God's kingdom come on earth as it is in heaven. "The Adventure of Jesus" has been used in the context of sending out missionaries, but the song also encompasses those who serve every day in their own communities. As Kevin notes, "We can all live the adventure where we're at." **Wherever you are, wherever God sends you, embrace all Jesus intends for you, serve others in need and live the adventure of Jesus.**

Prayer: Lift it Up

God who calls us from the safety of our boats, bid us to step out in faith. Breathe upon the embers of our devotion and fan them into flame. Forgive us for our apathy and complacency. Stir up fresh zeal and passion to serve You in this world. We want to be filled with the presence of Jesus and burn with passion for Him. We want to pray with His power and serve with His kindness. We seek to truly live the adventure of Jesus. Amen.

For Discussion: Talk it Out

1. How does sin cause the love of many to grow cold? Have you ever experienced coldness or spiritual sleepiness in your own life?

2. How can we heed God's warning and keep spiritually awake and alert?

3. What have you done to reach out in kindness within your city, as a witness of the love of Jesus?

Next Steps: Walk it Out

1. Memorize *Romans 12:11*

   "Do not be slothful in zeal, be fervent in spirit, serve the Lord."

   or *1 Corinthians 15:58.*

   "Therefore, my beloved brothers, be steadfast, immovable, always abounding in the work of the Lord, knowing that in the Lord your labor is not in vain."

2. Team up with another believer or another church for a synergistic ministry effort, whether it be writing a song, sharing the gospel, feeding the hungry or blessing your city on a larger scale.

3. Pray to be fully alive in the power of the Holy Spirit—to be sent by God into the mission of adventure for Him.

Here I am Lord

I, the Lord of sea and sky
I have heard My people cry
All who dwell in dark and sin
My hand will save
I, who made the stars of night
I will make their darkness bright
Who will bear My light to them?
Whom shall I send?

Here I am, Lord. Is it I, Lord?
I have heard You calling in the night
I will go, Lord, if You lead me
I will hold Your people in my heart

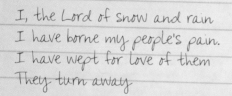

I, the Lord of snow and rain
I have borne my people's pain.
I have wept for love of them
They turn away

I will break their hearts of stone
Give them hearts for love alone
I will speak my words to them
Whom shall I send?

I will go where You lead me, Father lead me
I will go, I will follow, endlessly

Dan Schutte

Additional words and music by Chris Bray

14

Here I am Lord

And the Lord came and stood, calling as at other times, "Samuel! Samuel!" And Samuel said, "Speak, for your servant hears." – 1 Samuel 3:10

Called

Across the pages of Scripture, God calls out to His followers. Adam hears the call to come out of hiding. Noah hears the call to build. Abram hears the call to go. Moses hears the call to rescue. Samuel and Isaiah hear the call to speak as God's prophets. Across history, men and women have heard and responded to the voice of God. His call is surprising. Sometimes it comes in a burning bush, in the storm, or in the stillness. God's voice comes to each of us, today, through the pages of His Word as His Spirit applies truth to our hearts. It comes through creation where His magnificent glory is lavishly displayed for all to marvel at. What is our response when He calls?

Can we Hear?

Author Robert Velarde says, "Of all the human characters in the Chronicles of Narnia, Lucy is most attuned to Aslan's voice and calling. She hears him and obeys. Her faith opens her to the wonders of God and His calling."[1] Like Samuel, she awakens from her sleep, beckoned by the voice that calls her name. Many of us wish we could relate more to Lucy or Samuel. We find it difficult to hear God's voice, and no wonder; it's obscured by so many things. **The noise of our entertainment-filled world drowns out the whispers of God.** The plethora of electronic gadgets and unceasing screen time keeps our focus on the latest Facebook or Twitter updates rather than on spiritual reflection. Our breakneck pace of life keeps our hearts racing so fast that we've become unable to stop long enough to listen. Mercifully, the call of God is patient and persistent. Though we're hard of hearing, He continues to call our name and wait for our response.

> Learning to become quiet is important when it comes to hearing God's call. We need space for holy reflection.
>
> Robert Velarde [2]

Awakened and Surrendered

God's patient, persistent call came to Chris Bray through a song—a song he knew well. Chris grew up singing the song "Here I am Lord" at church, week after week. Years later, when he was questioning what he believed and searching for a personal faith, God used that familiar song to speak to him and turn his heart back towards the Father. Chris was reawakened to what true worship is: saying yes to God in all aspects of life. He came to a place of fresh surrender before God as he placed his all on the altar.

Since the days of his spiritual rebirth, this song has been a staple for Chris. He recorded it on his second worship CD and sings it whenever he leads people in worship. Because "Here I am Lord" was used so powerfully by God to call out a strong response from Chris, he was inspired to augment the song with a bridge, expressing his prayer of response. It was his "yes" to God. "I will go, where You lead me, Father lead me. I will go, I will follow endlessly."

As Chris leads this song of surrender, he's found that Jesus often touches people through it. Many times, those who have wandered away from the Lord will hear it and be drawn back to a time when they were closer to Him. In Chris's words: "The song's simplicity and honesty cannot only be felt in the hearts and minds of an adult but also a child, making it a useful and versatile tool for worship."

> Worship is the submission of all of our nature to God. It is the quickening of conscience by His holiness, nourishment of mind by His truth, purifying of imagination by His beauty, opening of the heart to His love, and submission of will to His purpose. And all this gathered up in adoration is the greatest of human expressions of which we are capable.
>
> Archbishop William Temple [3]

Third

One of Chris's favorite quotes comes from Catherine Doherty. As he considers what it means to live a life of worship and justice, Doherty's words "I am third," remind Bray that God must come first in our lives, our neighbour is second and we are in last place. This is how Chris strives to live. He admits, "When I first came to know the Lord, I was motivated by fear, and it was all about me. But as I started to learn more about this God I claimed to love, I started to realize the things that He is passionate about." As Chris read the gospels and meditated on the things that Jesus did—feeding the hungry, healing the sick, and ministering to the poor, he started to realize that there was more to life then the eternal endpoint; it's also the journey that matters.

Words that Challenge and Inspire

Two particular phrases in the song strike Chris whenever he sings it. The first is, "Here I am Lord." This line evokes the certainty of complete surrender. Chris says, "That can be scary, for we step out of our comfort zone and move towards something that might seem unsure, all the while trusting in God and His plan." The second phrase, just as challenging for Chris is: "I will go." He finds that, as believers, we often just talk about doing rather than actually taking action.

It is a challenge to hear God's voice. Do we long for it? Do we yearn to obey it? Do we run from it because of the implications of what follows once we hear? Isaiah said, *"And I heard the voice of the Lord saying "Whom shall I send, and who will go for us?" Then I said, "Here I am! Send me." (Isaiah 6:8)* Can we, will we respond like Isaiah? These are radical words. By saying them, like Isaiah, we are telling God we are completely His and will go anywhere He sends us and do anything He asks. Speak Lord, for your servant is listening.

Prayer: Lift it Up

Heavenly Father, help me hear and listen when You call my name. How grateful I am that You continue to speak and call out to me even though I am so apt not to hear or listen. Forgive me for being so dull of hearing. Speak life to me through Your Word, by Your Spirit, through Your creation and through Your people. Let me hear Your call and commission, as Isaiah did. Draw me out of sinful pride and fear and give me the courage to be fully surrendered to You and Your purposes for my life. **Searching God, who seeks those dwelling in dark and sin, use me to be Your voice of truth and grace to them.** Here I am, Lord. Amen.

For Discussion: Talk it Out

1. How did God's salvation call come to you? How quick were you to hear His voice?

2. What in your life obscures the voice of God from being heard?

3. Which of these two phrases is harder for you to pray, "Here I am," or "I will go"? Why?

Next Steps: Walk it Out

1. Grow your ability to hear God's voice by cultivating the discipline of setting aside specific times to listen.

2. Commit to listening for the voice of God as you're reading the Scriptures. Ask Him to speak through what you read, and to help you truly hear.

3. Repent of whatever is obscuring and hindering God's voice in your life.

4. Reflect on God's Word as you sit in silence. Record in a journal by writing or drawing what He speaks to you.

Lyrics: Brian McLaren
Music and Performance: Steve Bell

Kindness

Christ has no body here but ours
No hands no feet here on earth but ours.
Ours are the eyes through which He looks
On this world with kindness
Ours are the hands through which He works
Ours are the feet on which He moves
Ours are the voices through which He speaks
To this world with kindness
Through our touch, our smile, our listening ear
Embodied in us, Jesus is living here
Let us go now, inspirited
Into this world with kindness

Christ Has No Body
Teresa of Avila (1515–1582)

Christ has no body but yours,
No hands, no feet on earth but yours,
Yours are the eyes with which he looks
Compassion on this world,
Yours are the feet with which he walks to do good,
Yours are the hands, with which he blesses all the
world.
Yours are the hands, yours are the feet,
Yours are the eyes, you are his body.
Christ has no body now on earth but yours.

http://www.journeywithjesus.net/PoemsAndPrayers
/Teresa_Of_Avila_Christ_Has_No_Body.shtml
(accessed May 4, 2012)

15

Kindness

Thus says the Lord of hosts, Render true judgments,
show kindness and mercy to one another. – Zechariah 7:9

Who we Are

Christian. That's who we are. Richard Stearns asks, "What does that mean exactly? To even be Christians, we must first believe that Jesus Christ is the Son of God. That in itself is no small idea. **If it is true, it changes everything,** because if Christ is God, than all that He said and did is deeply significant to how we live our lives."[1]

We are all in process of understanding what it means "to be Christian"— what the Lord requires of us as we seek to understand doing justice, loving kindness, and walking humbly with our God. How we live our lives is to be characterized by the life of Jesus, "who went around doing good and healing all who were under the power of the devil, because God was with him" *(Acts 10:38).* We are called to live in the power of the Holy Spirit as Jesus lived and do as He did. Our charge, says Stearns, "Is to both proclaim and embody the gospel so that others can see, hear, and feel God's love in tangible ways."[2]

Hands and Feet

The song "Kindness" originated from the poem "Christ Has No Body" written by Teresa of Avila (1515–1582). The song and poem speak powerfully to us, as those who have the Spirit of God indwelling within, of our profound privilege and responsibility to physically embody Christ to the world in which He has placed us. It is both a startling and beautiful concept to grasp hold of: that the members of our bodies—these very hands, feet, and eyes we see before us—can actually act as a physical extension of Christ as God in His providence uses us.

Singer / songwriter Steve Bell wrote the music and put together the recording for "Kindness." Steve describes "Kindness" as a deceptively simple song. **"On its surface it is wonderfully hummable and nice. But at its core it is frighteningly revolutionary. No song has unsettled me more than this one."** "Kindness" challenges Steve at every level of his life and ministry, from how he shops, to how he eats, to how he moves about the planet, to how he interacts with his wife, kids, and neighbors. Steve testifies, "Ultimately, it challenges me with a gospel I have yet to fully accept. And so, it humbles me and forces me to my knees, begging mercy."

> I wanna be Your hands
> I wanna be Your feet
> I'll go where
> You send me
>
> Hands and Feet, Audio Adrenaline [3]

Seeing as Jesus Sees

Steve was deeply challenged when he went to the developing world in 1993. He was almost destroyed by the human suffering he witnessed on the streets of Calcutta. He found himself moved both by compassion and repulsion, and he was devastated by his own inability to respond in any way that seemed to actually matter. In the face of every suffering son, daughter, mother, father, brother, and sister, he saw the faces of his own and he couldn't imagine them suffering as these did.

Ten years later, on another trip to the Middle East he witnessed again the agony and suffering of displaced moms, dads, brothers and sisters. But this time, he didn't see the faces of his family superimposed on the faces of those he met. He experienced them as his own kin. He remembers, "That was a far more difficult experience that has never left me. How can I abandon MY mother, MY father, MY children to that suffering?" Steve returned home and realized that he was slowly becoming the Christian he had professed himself to be thirty years earlier. He recounts, "With that soul conversion comes the increasing inability to distinguish between "them" and "us." I was actually becoming a child of THE Father." Steve hopes this song will help people to realize that the faith we claim will eventually demand us to either abandon the faith itself, or relinquish our narrowly defined notion of family. The gospel is radical and demanding. He says, "What Trinitarian faith offers us is an inescapable vulnerability to the suffering of all humanity, and indeed all of creation. I don't think most of us have realized what we've signed on to."

Love in Action

Steve was impacted by Rodney Stark's book *The Rise of Christianity*.[4] Stark shows that there were two unique beliefs separating Christianity from the myriad of first century religious cults. These two concepts eventually undermined the Roman Empire and brought paganism to near extinction. The first belief was, God loves the world, and the second, you can't please God without loving what God loves.

In his book, Stark recounts a compelling story from the early second century. A devastating plague swept through the port cities of the Mediterranean where the tiny, fledgling Christian communities were scattered. While the elite fled the cities and abandoned the overcrowded poor to their miserable fates, the Christians stayed behind and tended to the sick at the risk of their own lives. Why did they do this? Because God loves the world and you can't please God without loving what God loves.

As it turned out, in the second century, if there happened to be Christians living in your neighborhood when a plague struck, you had a statistically higher chance of surviving. These early Christians saw no division between acts of worship and acts of compassion and justice. Moved by the heart of God, they stepped out, at great risk, as the eyes, hands and feet of Jesus. Steve believes a day is coming when Christians in the Western world will be called upon to make a choice of how they will respond to the desperate—just as in the second century. In his words, "We are going to have to face the gospel squarely and either embrace or dismiss. We're coming to a mettle testing moment."

Send Me

Each time the Church gathers should be a time of facing God and the gospel squarely. The church gathers to worship and be taught, and the church scatters to worship and serve. Believers are gathered together to be sent out. Through the pages of this book we have gathered around scriptures, songs and stories and in them have been brought face to face with the mercy, justice and love of God. Having gathered together over these words of instruction and conviction, now we are to be sent out. We are now filled to pour out. The final lyrics of this song say, "Let us go now, inspirited, into this world with kindness." Inspirited means instilled with courage. This courage comes from the promise and power of God.

God sends a benediction upon His "going" Church. He promises to bless us and keep us, make His face to shine upon us, be gracious to us, lift up His countenance upon us, and give us peace *(Numbers6:24-26)*. He assures us that the grace of the Lord Jesus Christ, the love of God, and the fellowship of the Holy Spirit will be with us all as we go to be His people and do His work *(2 Cor.13:14).* **We are sent to go into the world to love and serve the Lord.** We are sent out by God to engage this world, shine His light, incarnate His merciful presence, faithfully proclaim the gospel, and lead people to a saving knowledge of Jesus Christ.

In these "go and serve the Lord" benedictions, we continue to see that worship leads us to action and our action is the worship lived out in sacrificial service. We are fully surrendered to Christ. We will follow. We will be His eyes, His hands, His feet.

Prayer: Lift it Up

Lord of Compassion who frees the captives, we praise You for life eternal. We have been freed from a life of living for self and we are captive to the call to follow You. We are Your hands. We are Your feet. We thank You for the Body of Christ, the Church, for each of its members, living representations of You. Use these hands, feet, voices, and eyes, to see as You see, do as You do, and go where You lead. Inspirited, empowered by Your grace, send us, Lord, to be Your eyes, hands, feet and voice of truth. Amen.

For Discussion: Talk it Out

1. Read *Hebrews 13:16*. Are you ever tempted to give up on "doing good"? Why? How does understanding doing good as a sacrifice to God change your perspective on acts of goodness and kindness?

2. How do the words of "Kindness" and "Christ Has No Body" impact you?

3. Discuss the power of a benediction in a worship service. How does "Now go into the world to love and serve the Lord" focus you in being the hands and feet of Jesus?

Next Steps: Walk it Out

1. Be exposed to the call to be Jesus' hands and feet as you read *The Hole In Our Gospel* by Richard Stearns, or *When Necessary Use Words* by Mike Pilavachi.

2. "You can't please God without loving what God loves." Do a Bible study on what God loves and pray that, in an increasing measure, you grow in living out the love of Christ.

3. If you are a church leader, examine your theology of the benediction and evaluate how effective your practice is for the sending out of your people.

ANSWER THE CALL

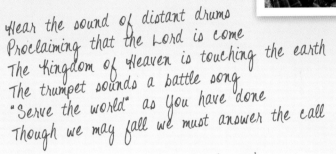

Hear the sound of distant drums
Proclaiming that the Lord is come
The Kingdom of Heaven is touching the earth
The trumpet sounds a battle song
"Serve the world" as you have done
Though we may fall we must answer the call

To bring healing where there's pain
To the broken and ashamed
Be the voice of truth where there is injustice
To the orphaned and the lost
Be the message of the cross
Though we may fall we must answer the call

See your plans of love unfold
Redeeming lives across the world
Our voices tell your story for all to hear
A Saviour in a manger laid
And how the price of sin was paid
Though we may fall we must answer the call

Steve Mitchinson

16

Answer the Call

For even the Son of Man came not to be served but to serve, and to give his life as a ransom for many. – Mark 10:43b-45

Greatness, Jesus Style

Greatness. Who doesn't want to have a great life? But what defines greatness? This is an important question. Is it having a great portfolio, a great family and friends? Or is it something else? We know how greatness is understood by much of the corporate world and entertainment industry, but what is biblical greatness? Philip Greenslade writes, "In a radical fashion, Jesus, by example and word, establishes servanthood as the way in which his men are to lead others."[1] Greatness is lived out servanthood. It is being a faithful steward of the gifts and call of God. **Jesus did not rebuke His disciples for seeking to be great, He simply redefined true greatness.** Jesus said, *"I am among you as the one who serves." (Luke 22:27)* Servanthood is the road less traveled; the one that puts others ahead of ourselves. Are we still excited about greatness, as defined by Jesus' life and teaching?

Summoned to Serve

Steve Mitchinson finds himself stepping into many roles, and his desire is to have a servant's heart in each area of his life. He's a husband, father, songwriter, worship leader, and Palliative Care physician. Steve wrote the song "Answer The Call" as a summons to the Church of Jesus Christ to respond to Christ, the Suffering Servant, in laying down our lives like He did. Bishop Graham Cray says, "It was never intended that we should share in the Son's fellowship with the Father if we don't also share in the Son's mission from the Father. We become the bridge people, joining a broken and lost world to the broken heart of God."[2] Steve has found himself on a mission, seeking to be a "bridge person," and inspired by *Mark 10:43-44: "But whoever would be great among you must be your servant, and whoever would be first among you must be slave of all."*

The War of Love

"Answer The Call" conveys a sense of the urgency of the mission. The song reminds us that we are at war against the enemy of souls, who seeks to destroy life and turn hearts away from God. The drums of war give us cadence for our advancement. The blast of the trumpet calls us to rise up as God's warriors to serve the broken and lost. Our mission is:

To bring healing where there's pain
To the broken and ashamed
Be the voice of truth where there is injustice
To the orphaned and the lost
Be the message of the cross

As John Stott says, when we look out on the gross injustices that occur in every corner of the globe, we should not ask, "'What is wrong with the world?' for that diagnosis has already been given. Rather, we should ask, 'What has happened to the salt and light?'"[3] We are the ones meant to fight against the darkness as salt and light. We are in a battle, and our weapons are mighty. God's presence, His truth, and His compassion are ours as we step forward in response to His voice. Will we answer His call to something greater than ourselves? Will we offer up the sacrifice of our lives to His kingdom?

Beyond Our Comfort Zone

In Steve's vocation and through his music he seeks to live in sacrifice for the suffering and dispossessed, as the hands and voice of Jesus. He's living out this call as a Palliative Care physician who works with those approaching the end of their physical lives. He has seen how God pursues His children to their very last breath and considers it a great privilege to come alongside the dying. In the valley of the shadow of death, Steve seeks to bring the light of Jesus. "Answer The Call" continues to be an inspiration for Steve in that it challenges him to go beyond what's comfortable, by setting his own comforts aside in service to those experiencing many levels of pain.

> God is totally involved in His world, but He has chosen to get His hands dirty through ours, if we are willing to make them available.
>
> Graham Kendrick [4]

Music That Ministers

When we think of worship and justice, rarely do we consider the elderly and the ill who are looking straight into the end of their lives. Often these people are forgotten and lonely. Steve knows that we in the West have become adept at avoiding the issues surrounding death and dying. He says maybe it is "because those roads lead us to a sense of our own human frailty and the fragility of human life."

Steve feels strongly that music has an important part to play in pallia-tive care. He says, **"Pain (in whatever format it comes) is what happens to the body, suffering is what happens to the person. Music can bring great comfort to those at a time of great need, loss and suffering.** It has a way of touching and releasing our emotions that goes beyond our abilities to communicate in more conventional ways." To this end, Steve recently released *Giver of Life*, a new CD he hopes will bring some hope and com-fort to those that find themselves facing their own death and to those who are caring for them as friends and family. This has been done through The Gracenote Project, a non-profit organization set up to resource spiritual care for those encountering the process of dying.[5]

Serving in His Sufficiency

Though we may fall we must answer the call. Answering the call of Jesus with a wholehearted "yes" means we have faced our fears and con-sidered the cost. "Answer The Call" addresses the fear that we have as we seek to live as God's agents of mercy and grace. Like the twelve spies of *Numbers 13* who were called to survey the land, we feel outnumbered and outsized. We feel inadequate and insignificant. Yet with the humility and the childlike faith that Jesus commended as greatness in

> Ministry takes place when divine resources meet human needs through loving channels to the glory of God.
>
> Warren Wiersbe [6]

the kingdom of heaven[7] we respond like Caleb who exclaimed in resolute trust in the power of God, *"Let us go up at once and take possession, for we are well able to overcome it"* (Numbers 13:30).

In the face of overwhelming circumstances, God promises to be our sufficiency. His arm is not too short. He is the God of the impossible. As we step forward, willing to take risks as His servants, we will see His plans of love unfold and we will have the privilege of partnering in

His work of redemption. He waits to pour His divine resources through surrendered servants to meet every aching need.

Prayer: Lift it Up

Lord Jesus Christ, servant of all, You call us away from dreams that are too small to Your greater mission of reaching this broken world in Your name. **Forgive us Lord, for we have misunderstood greatness. Forgive us Lord for we have sought to be served rather than serve.** You have shown us that greatness is found in humility and a surrendered life of service for You. Invited into Your mission, we are compelled to leave our spaces of comfort and trust You for the strength to love those You love. Touch the dying, the elderly, the lonely and forgotten. Use us, Lord. We will answer Your call. Amen.

For Discussion: Talk it Out

1. How do you define greatness? How is this lived out in your life?

2. Believers can get distracted from the clarity of the mission by any number of fads or distractions. What distracts you? How do you understand the mission of Jesus?

3. Graham Kendrick says, "God is totally involved in His world, but He has chosen to get His hands dirty through ours, if we are willing to make them available."[8] Are you willing, as God's servant, to get your hands dirty? What can we learn from Caleb in *Numbers 13?*

Next Steps: Walk it Out

1. As a physician and musician, Steve is combining his skills and abilities to serve the needy. What are your skills and abilities? How are you putting these to work for the needy?

2. Dr. Bob Pierce said, "Don't fail to do something just because you can't do everything."[9] What is a something you can do tomorrow?

3. Do you know someone who is approaching the end of physical life? Visit them and bring the light of Jesus in the shadows of their last days.

The next step
is yours...

1. This is Our Love

1. Timothy Keller, Generous Justice: How God's Grace Makes Us Just, New York: Dutton, 2010

2. You are Good

1. John Piper - http://www.desiringgod.org/iphone/dwyl/book/chapter3.html Accessed April 12, 2012

2. Thomas Merton - http://www.goodreads.com/quotes/show/135240. Accessed April 10, 2012.

3. AW Tozer – The Knowledge of the Holy, http://kjos1.securesites.net/Excerpts/books/faith/Tozer/tozer-knowledge.htm

4. http://www.goodreads.com/quotes/show/135240. Accessed April 10, 2012.

3. From You for You

1. A.W. Tozer http://oakhillministries.org/archives/To%20Be%20Understood,%20Truth%20Must%20Be%20Lived.pdf   Accessed April 25, 2012

2. Paul Carter – from a sermon For Our Good Always, First Baptist church, Orillia, ON June 17, 2102

3. Discussion question 1 – A.W. Tozer quote. http://www.cmalliance.org/devotions/tozer?id=573, Accessed June 5, 2012

4. Something to Give

1. Mary Maxwell. Channels Only – Public Domain (from Hymn Book)

2. NT Wright - Quoted by Carolyn Arends, and referenced in this sermon http://ntwrightpage.com/sermons/EasterVigil09.htm

5. Defender of the Poor

1. The Great Awakening – Leeland Mooring , Essential Records © 2011

2. Steve Bell as Quoted by Mike Janzen

6.   Light of the World

1. Mike Pilavachi pull quote Regal books Venture, CA, 2006, p. 10
   http://books.google.ca/books?id=PKnaqlxpStMC&pg=PA10&lpg=PA10&dq#v=o
   nepage&q&f=false

7.   Revive us Again

1. Andy Park, The Art of Compassion, New York: Faith Words, 2009, 141.

2. Ibid., 139.

3. Mark Labberton -The Dangerous Act of Worship: Living God's Call To Justice
   (Downers Grove: IVP), 2007. http://books.google.ca/books?id=UFZMJ_G20_EC
   &pg=PA38&lpg=PA38&dq#v=onepage&q&f=false

4. see http://www.compassionart.tv for further information on CompassionArt

5. Dave Toycen – From an interview conducted on Feb. 14, 2012

6. Andy Park, The Art of Compassion, New York: Faith Words, 2009, 156

7. Ibid, 149

8.   Break my Heart

1. Richard Foster, Celebration of Discipline, (San Francisco: HarperCollins),
   1978, 33.

2. Acts 8:9-24

3. http://www.nouwenlegacy.com/in_the_name_comments.pdf.
   Accessed May 10, 2012

4. Henri Nouwen, In The Name of Jesus, New York: Crossroad, 1996. 59.

5. ibid

9.   Children of the World

1. Richard Stearns, The Hole In Our Gospel, Nashville: Nelson, 2009, 107.

2. http://www.globalissues.org/article/26/poverty-facts-and-stats.
   Accessed May 15, 2012

3. http://www.ijm.org/our-work/injustice-today

4. http://www.goodreads.com/author/quotes/4837.Henri_J_M_Nouwen.
   Accessed May 3, 2012

10. Real Life Offering

1. Kevin Deyoung and Greg Gilbert, What Is the Mission of the Church? © 2011, Wheaton: Crossway, p. 155.

11. Least of These

1. David Ruis, The Justice God is Seeking, Ventura: Regal, 2006, 10.

2. David Ruis, The Justice God is Seeking, Ventura: Regal, 2006, 58.

12. Break God's Heart

13. The Adventure of Jesus

1. Matthew 24:12

2. Kevin Boese/Brian Doerksen - From song lyrics

14. Here I Am

1. http://www.focusonthefamily.com/faith/spiritual_development/attuning_to_gods_presence_and_calling.aspx. Accessed May 10, 2012.

2. ibid

3. Archbishop William Temple - http://www.worshipmatters.com/2005/11/04/defining-worship/, Accessed June 3, 2012

15. Kindness

1. Richard Stearns, The Hole In Our Gospel, Nashville: Nelson, 2009, 1.

2. Ibid, 18.

3. Audio Adrenaline Hands and Feet - Track 6 on Underdog CD 1999, Forefront Records, written by: Mark Stuart, Bob Herdman, Will McGuiness, Tyler Burkhum, and Charlie Peacock.

4. Rodney Stark, The Rise of Christianity, San Francisco: HarperCollins, 1997.

16. Answer the Call

1. Philip Greenslade, Leadership, Greatness and Servanthood, Minneapolis: Bethany House, 1984, 3.

2. Graham Cray, The Art of Compassion, New York: FaithWords, 2009, 225.

3. John Stott - http://dailychristianquote.com/dcqwitness.html. Accessed May 13, 2012

4. Graham Kendrick, The Art of Compassion, New York: FaithWords, 2009, 164.

5. For more information about Giver of Life and Steve's ministry go to www.gracenoteproject.com

6. Warren Wiersbe, On Being A Servant of God, Grand Rapids: Baker, 1993, 3.

7. Matthew 18:4

8. (Graham Kendrick quote in discussion question 3) Graham Kendrick, The Art of Compassion, New York: FaithWords, 2009, 164

9. Bob Pierce (quote in Next steps questions 2) In The Hole In Our Gospel: The Answer That Changed My Life and Might Just Change the World by Richard Stearns, p. 152

Ali Matthews
www.alimatthews.com

Stratford, Ontario's Ali Matthews has been a performing songwriter since her teens. She has released six critically acclaimed albums and received numerous awards including 14 GMA Covenant Awards. Ali's heart is to write songs that draw people closer to grace, to each other, and to our Creator.

Andy Park
www.andypark.ca

Andy is a worship leader, songwriter, and pastor. In addition to his many worship songs, (including "In the Secret") Andy has also authored two books. He resides in Surrey, British Columbia, where he's co-leading a church plant and continuing in itinerant ministry.

Brad Guldemond
www.bradguld.com

Brad is currently the music and creative arts pastor at Gateway Alliance Church in Edmonton, Alberta. Brad's passion is to see people have a relationship with God that overflows into loving others and living a lifestyle of worship.

Carolyn Arends
www.carolynarends.com

British Columbia's Carolyn Arends has released ten award-winning albums and authored two books. In addition to her concert and speaking schedule, she is a wife, mother, college instructor, grad student, and columnist for Christianity Today.

Chris Bray

www.chrisbraymusic.com

Chris is a worship leader from Aylmer, Ontario, where he lives with his wife Katie and three children. His passion for our response to God's call has led him across North America, sharing with thousands his music, testimony, heart for social justice and love for God.

Dan Macaulay

www.danmacaulay.com

Dan is an award-winning Canadian worship leader, songwriter, recording artist and World Vision advocate. Dan currently lives with his wife and young son in Greenwich, Connecticut, where he serves as Worship Pastor of Harvest Time Church, in addition to travelling internationally for teaching and worship ministry.

Downhere

www.downhere.com

Downhere is a Juno, Dove, and Covenant Award winning Canadian Christian rock band living in Nashville, Tennessee. They are committed to using their gifts to reaffirm and shore up the foundations of the faith.

Jacob Moon

www.jacobmoon.com

Jacob, singer and songwriter of award-winning pop and folk songs from Hamilton, Ontario, is known, in particular, for his live shows featuring his command of the guitar, and "live looping." It's onstage that Jacob's compositions take flight, and his listeners are swept up in the jetstream.

Jill Hagen
www.jillhagen.com

A singer / songwriter and worship director from Camrose, Alberta, Jill has been in full time music ministry since September 2008. In travelling across North America to perform, she hopes to inspire listeners to "live different from the ordinary" by following God's heart for those in need.

Jody Cross
www.jodycross.com

Jody serves as worship pastor at First Baptist Church in Orillia, Ontario, where he is developing a worship culture and training worship leaders. Jody also leads worship seminars to equip worship leaders and churches to experience the transformational power and presence of God in corporate worship.

Kevin Boese
www.kevinboese.com

Kevin leads worship at Fresh Wind Christian Fellowship and MB Mission. He resides in Abbotsford, British Columbia with his beautiful wife Nancy and four amazing kids, and when not spending time with his family or guitar he's probably careening down a gnarly trail on his mountain bike.

Mike Janzen
www.mikejanzen.ca;
www.monsoonworship.com

Mike works as a freelance pianist / composer and lives in Toronto, Ontario, with his wife Jodi and daughter Hadassah. He leads worship at Little Trinity Anglican Church, and he heads up an award winning jazz trio, which recently played Massey Hall with Steve Bell and the Toronto Symphony.

Sean Dayton

www.seandayton.com

Sean is an award winning worship leader from North Bay, Ontario. He and his wife, Aimee, have released four albums, and his songs can be heard on radio stations across Canada. Sean and Aimee are artist associates for Food For The Hungry.

Starfield

www.starfieldonline.com

Canadian worship band Starfield has spent the last ten years partnering with churches and ministries in leading various groups in passionate and energetic worship. Starfield-penned songs like "Filled With Your Glory," "Reign In Us," and "The Saving One" are sung in church services every weekend all over the world.

Steve Bell

www.stevebell.com

Award winning Winnipeg, Manitoba-based singer/songwriter Steve Bell has enjoyed success over a prolific solo career that has spanned two decades. Steve has produced 15 albums throughout these years, albums that have resonated deeply within the hearts of his listeners.

Steve Mitchinson

www.gracenoteproject.com

Steve is a GP doctor, currently training as a palliative care physician. He is also a singer / songwriter / worship leader, having three albums recorded and a number of songs published. Steve currently lives near Vancouver, BC.

Song Selection Committee

To Our Song Selection Committee

We'd like recognize those who served on our song selection committee. Each person was challenged to evaluate and rank the 33 finalist songs. Based on their feedback the top 16 songs emerged and are featured on this CD and devotional guide.

Andrea Tisher	**First Baptist Church,** Vancouver, BC
Ann Chow	**Knox Church,** Toronto, ON
Bert Steingard	**Harvest Bible Chapel,** Barrie, ON
Bev Foster	**Room 217,** Port Perry, ON
Brock Tozer	**CHRI 99.1 FM,** Ottawa, ON
Carla Yorke	**First Baptist Church,** Orillia, ON
Chris Vacher	**Orangeville Baptist Church,** Orangeville, ON
Chris Westby	**Regina Apostolic Church,** Regina, SK
Dawn Woodland	**Harvest Bible Chapel,** Barrie, ON
Drew Brown	**Trinity Anglican,** Streetsville, ON

Geoff Dresser	**Grant Memorial Church,** Winnipeg, MB
George McEachern	**Crossroads Communications,** Burlington, ON
Hiram Joseph	**The People's Church,** Toronto, ON
Jason Erhardt	**First Alliance Church,** Calgary, ON
Jill Kozak	**Smythe Street Cathedral,** Fredericton, NB
John Williams	**Tenth Ave. Alliance,** Vancouver, BC
Johnny Markin	**Northview Church,** Abbotsford, BC
Jonathan Gonyou	**Stony Plain Alliance Church,** Stony Plain, AB
Joshua Seller	**Harvest Bible Chapel,** Oakville, ON
Justin Bradbury	**Southlands Community Church,** Winnipeg, MB
Karlene Fletcher	**Whitby Free Methodist Church ,** Whitby, ON
Kevin Loten	**Iris Mission,** Malawi, Africa
Levi Denbok	**First Baptist Church,** Stayner, ON
Lyle and Jean Buyer	**McKernan Baptist Church,** Edmonton, AB
Martin Smith	**David C. Cook,** Vancouver, BC
Melissa McEachern	**Crossroads Communications,** Burlington, ON
Margaret Ellen Horrocks	**Cambridge Vineyard,** Kitchener, ON
Paul Elliott	**Music Professional,** St. Thomas, ON
Pearl Dresser	**Grant Memorial Church,** Winnipeg, MB
Ron Weber	**World Vision Canada,** Mississauga, ON
Scott Jackson	**Life 100.3 FM,** Barrie, ON
Stephen White	**Salvation Army,** Toronto, ON
Tim Schwindt	**River Music Productions,** London, ON
Wendy Porter	**McMaster Divinity College,** Hamilton, ON
Woody Woodland	**Harvest Bible Chapel,** Barrie, ON

ARTIST	SONG TITLE	ALBUM NAME
Ali Matthews	Break God's Heart	*Carry Me Home*
Andy Park	Revive us Again	*Unshakable*
Brad Guldemond Performed by Elevate	Real Life Offering	*Elevate*
Carolyn Arends	Something to Give	*Pollyanna's Attic*
Chris Bray	Here I am Lord	*Let Hope Arise*
Dan Macaulay	From You for You	*From You For You*
Downhere	Break my Heart	*B-Sides*
Jacob Moon	Children of the World	*Maybe Sunshine*
Jill Hagen	Least of These	*Ruined for the Ordinary*
Jody Cross	This is Our Love	
Kevin Boese	The Adventure of Jesus	*One*
Mike Janzen	Defender of the Poor	*Little Trinity Sessions*
Sean Dayton	You are Good	*Hear The Sound*
Starfield	Light of the World	*The Kingdom*
Steve Bell	Kindness	*Kindness*
Steve Mitchinson	Answer the Call	*War of Love*

Each artist and record label has generously given permission for their song to be used royalty free. Proceeds from this product will go to support the ministries of World Vision Canada and Crossroads Christian Communications.

SONG AUTHOR	COPYRIGHT	PRODUCER
Ali Matthews	©2010 Shake-a-Paw music	Ali Matthews and Rick Francis
Andy Park	©2006 ION Publishing	Nathan Nockels
Brad Guldemond	©2004 Brad Guldemond	Ken Dosso
Carolyn Arends	©2006 Running Arends Music/(p) 2B Music	Carolyn Arends and Roy Salmond
Written by Dan Schutte. (Additional words and music by Chris Bray. A LicenSingOnline license is needed to reprint this material visit wwww.licensingonline.org.)	Text and Music ©1981 OCP; Additional words and music ©2011 Chris Bray	Andrew Horrocks
Dan Macaulay	©2010 Dan Macaulay Music	Keith Everette Smith
Jason Germain and Marc Martel	©2008 Centricity Music	
Jacob Moon	©2009 Jacob Moon	Jacob Moon
Jill Hagen	©2010 Jill Hagen	Roy Salmond
Jody Cross, Travis Doucette and Drew Brown	© 2012 Window Into Worship / Red Tie Music, ASCAP	Andrew Horrocks
Kevin Boese and Brian Doerksen	©2001 ION Publishing	Philip Janz
Mike Janzen	©2009 Mike Janzen /Monsoon Music	
Sean Dayton & Brent Milligan	©2010 Sean Dayton & Brent Milligan	Brent Milligan
Tim Neufeld, Jon Neufeld & Allen Salmon	©2012 Neufeld Music	Allen Salmon
Brian McLaren	©2011 Signpost Music (Master) ©Brian McLaren (Music & Lyrics)	Steve Bell, Dave Zeglinski, Murray Pulver
Steve Mitchinson	©2007 ION Records	Philip Janz

World Vision

For Children. For Change. For Life.

World Vision is a Christian relief, development and advocacy organization dedicated to working with children, families and communities to overcome poverty and injustice. As followers of Jesus, we are motivated by God's love for all people regardless of race, religion, gender or ethnicity.

www.churches.worldvision.ca

crossroads
LIFE-CHANGING MEDIA

Crossroads Christian Communications is Canada's leader in providing faith and values media content for people of all ages. Their mandate is to expand the impact of God's message of love and hope using the power of media. www.crossroads.ca

With Contributions by:

GRAF-MARTIN
communications inc.

Graf-Martin Communications Inc. - Project design and coordination.

AME Recording Studio - CD assembly and mastering.

To download chord sheets for these songs visit www.jodycross.com.

For more information on this project visit
www.churches.worldvision.ca/thisisourlove.